W9-APW-786

Thank you

Anna Bergenström, who checked our facts;
Professor Leif Hambraeus (Uppsala University),
who reviewed the pages on nutrition;
Friends of the Earth, who looked over the chapter
on world food production;
and Birgitta Gustafson (agricultural journalist),
who checked the section on cows and hens

Rabén & Sjögren Stockholm

Translation copyright © 1990 by Joan Sandin
All rights reserved
Illustrations copyright © 1980 by Lena Anderson
Originally published in Sweden by Rabén & Sjögren
under the title *Linus bakar och lagar,*
copyright © 1980 by Christina Björk
Photographs: p. 13: Rune Olsson; p. 14: C. V. Roikjer, Photo-
grapher for the King; p. 16: Stig A. Nilsson; p. 17: Horst
Tuuloskorpi; p. 22: Skokloster; p. 43: Emil Schulthess; p. 52:
The Nordic Museum; p. 57 (the dog): after Johan Gustaf von
Holst's painting *A Scholar.*
Library of Congress catalog card number: 89-63051
Printed in Italy
First edition, 1990

R & S Books are distributed
in the United States of America by Farrar, Straus and Giroux, New York;
in the United Kingdom by Ragged Bears, Andover;
in Canada by Vanwell Publishing, St. Catharines
and in Australia by ERA Publications, Adelaide

ISBN 91 29 59658 0

Elliot's Extraordinary Cookbook

Text by Christina Björk
Pictures by Lena Anderson
Translated by Joan Sandin

My name is Elliot.
Before you start reading this book, I'd like to say a few things:

- I've shortened some words in the recipes, like this:

tablespoon = tbsp.
teaspoon = tsp.
ounce = oz.
pound = lb.

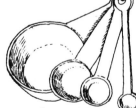

- I always measure my ingredients with measuring spoons or a measuring cup.
- When it says butter, you can use margarine instead if you want to. But make sure the margarine is the right kind for cooking and baking (fat content at least 80 percent). You *can't* use soft "table spreads."
- One more thing: Before I start cooking, I wash my hands.

R&S
BOOKS

I forget my

What we did with the potatoes

First Stella peeled four large potatoes. Then I grated them on a cheese grater (using the side with the biggest holes). I had to be careful not to grate my fingers. The last little piece was impossible to grate, so I ate it instead. (Raw potatoes don't taste all that bad.)

When the potatoes were grated, Stella covered them with a double paper towel and pressed out the "juice" with her hand.

Stella had a small iron frying pan. We put some butter in it and heated it up on the stove. When the butter had melted and stopped sputtering, we quickly put in the grated potatoes. We added a little salt and some crushed leaves of an herb called *basil*.

"And now I'll turn down the heat," said Stella, "so it doesn't burn."

We let the potatoes cook slowly for about five minutes. Then we turned over the pancake with a pancake turner. We sprinkled some salt and basil on the other side, too; it was all nice and golden brown now.

Five more minutes and the potato pancake was ready to eat. It tasted UNBELIEVABLY good! Imagine, just a few potatoes . . .

When I got home I wrote in my notebook: Tuesday: Forgot my key. Went up to Stella's. Made a potato pancake.

O ne day I forgot my key and had to sit out on the steps to wait for somebody to come home. I figured I was in for a long wait, but then someone came. It was Mrs. Delight, who lives upstairs.

"You poor child," she said, "sitting on that cold stairway."

"I forgot my key," I said.

"Well then, come on up to my place and wait there. My name is Stella. What's yours?"

"Elliot Nelson," I said.

Stella's apartment was nice, with lots of things to look at. I thought the most interesting thing was a bottle with a little boat in it.

"That's the boat we worked on, Archie and I," said Stella. "I was the cook and Archie worked up on deck."

"Where is Archie now?" I asked.

"He got washed overboard in a storm," said Stella. "We never found him, my poor Archie. This is what he looked like." She pointed to the photograph beside the bottle.

How sad, I thought. Poor Stella, what if she starts crying now that she's reminded of Archie . . .

But instead she said, "Are you hungry, Elliot? Go see what you can find in the pantry."

"There's nothing but a bag of potatoes in here," I said.

"What luck!" said Stella. "If you have nothing but some potatoes and a dab of butter, you're all set for a feast."

Oh sure, I thought. But that was *before* . . .

Stella Delight's Special

POTATO PANCAKE FOR TWO:

4 LARGE POTATOES, PEELED AND GRATED (SQUEEZE OUT SOME OF THE "JUICE")

2 TBSP. BUTTER FOR FRYING

1/2 TSP. SALT

1/2 TSP. CRUSHED BASIL

FLATTEN AND FRY 5 MINUTES ON EACH SIDE.

key and meet Stella

STELLA KNOWS A LOT ABOUT FOOD. THIS WASN'T THE ONLY THING
SHE TAUGHT ME ABOUT POTATOES. TURN THE PAGE AND YOU'LL SEE...

A POTATO
"EYE"
WHERE
A SPROUT
CAN GROW

THIS IS A MEDIUM - SIZE
POTATO (I THINK)

We make Earth Apples in Field Jackets

"Do you know how to make Earth Apples in Field Jackets?" Stella asked me one day. "That's a dish that was served at the court of the French king several hundred years ago."

"Sounds pretty fancy," I said. "What is it?"

"It's boiled potatoes in their skins," said Stella.

"Is that all," I said. "That's easy enough to make."

"Not as easy as you think," said Stella.

Here's what we did:

First we picked out potatoes that were all about the same size. That way they'll cook in about the same amount of time. (It takes longer for the heat to go through a big potato.)

We washed the potatoes well with water and a scrub brush. Then we put them in a pot and filled it with water, covering all the potatoes.

"You should really cook vegetables in boiling water," said Stella. "But we'll use cold water so we won't burn ourselves. Potatoes always seem to plop and splash when you put them into hot water."

We put a lid on the pot and set it on the stove to cook.

"Aren't you supposed to salt the water?" I asked.

"No, there's no reason to do that," said Stella. "The salt can't get through the skins anyway."

After that we just waited for the water to start boiling. First there were some small bubbles in the bottom of the pot.

"That's the steam trying to get up to the surface," said Stella. "When there are lots of small bubbles, the water is *simmering*. When there are lots of bigger bubbles, the water has reached 212 degrees Fahrenheit, and it is *boiling*."

When the water started boiling, we turned down the heat.

"It won't go any faster if it's *boiling over*," said Stella. "Potatoes cook better at a slow boil, when the water is about 200 degrees."

"And that saves energy, too," I said. "How long should the potatoes cook?"

DO THEY FEEL SOFT NOW?

"POMMES DE TERRE EN ROBE DES CHAMPS" IS WHAT THEY'RE CALLED IN FRENCH

tuber

"We can check them after fifteen minutes," said Stella, "but they usually take about twenty minutes. *Overcooked* potatoes are not that good."

What does "cooked" mean?

"Why do they get soft?" I asked.

"I'll try to explain," said Stella. "The 'meat' of the potato is divided into small rooms called cells. You'd have to look through a microscope to see them. Potato cells have hard walls, which is why raw potatoes are so hard.

"When a potato gets warm, the hard cell walls become soft and separate from each other. Then the potato feels soft and tastes good. And that's when our stomachs are able to digest them."

"Maybe *you* should check it, too," I told Stella, after I'd stuck a matchstick into one of the potatoes.

"This potato isn't warm enough inside yet," she said. "It should feel a *little* softer than this."

Five minutes more and our potatoes were done. Stella drained off the water.

"Now they can sit and let off some steam, so they'll get really nice and dry," said Stella.

"There's lots of vitamin C just inside the peel," she added.

"Then it was *lucky* that we didn't peel them," I said.

"That's right," said Stella. "If you peel potatoes before you cook them, many of the vitamins will get thrown away with the water. But now it's time to eat . . ."

We each speared a potato with a fork and carefully peeled it. It was easy; the peel was like a fine thin silk cloth. Then we each put a pat of butter and some salt on our potatoes.

"Wow!" I said. "It's amazing that a potato can taste so good *all by itself*! When I eat potatoes with other food, I never even notice how they taste."

"But then, not all potatoes are cooked this well," said Stella. "A lot of people don't bother making Earth Apples in Field Jackets the right way."

The history of the potato (as told by Stella)

South American Indians were the ones who first discovered that potatoes could be planted and eaten. They called them *papas.*

We think the first potatoes came to Europe on Spanish ships returning from the New World about 500 years ago. They were brought to North America in the early 1600s. Today most of the world's potatoes are grown in the Soviet Union.

At first people were suspicious of the new vegetable. This was partly because everything that grows *above* the ground on a potato plant is poisonous. Who could believe that those bumpy things growing *under* the ground could be so delicious, and good for you, and cheap to grow. (Potatoes that grow *above ground* and turn green are poisonous.) It took a while before people became convinced, but now the potato is the world's most widely grown vegetable and one of our most important foods.

Solanum tuberosum
THE POTATO'S LATIN NAME

Imagine, a single potato can produce forty new potatoes the next year! The potato plant is a relative of the tomato and the tobacco plant.

I've learned a few more potato recipes from Stella. Sometimes Arthur visits Stella with me. Arthur is pretty picky about food: nothing spicy or sour or hard to chew or with bones. But he usually likes Stella's cooking, even though he *really* only likes hot dogs and spaghetti.

Mashed Potatoes

They're good with ham or fish.

HERE'S WHAT YOU'LL NEED FOR TWO HUNGRY PEOPLE:

6 medium-size potatoes
2/3 cup milk
1 tbsp. butter (or a bit more)
Some salt
Some chopped parsley

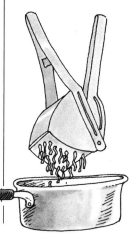

HERE'S WHAT YOU DO:

• Boil the potatoes the way we did before. Peel them. (Or peel them before you boil them.)

• Mash the potatoes in a pan. It's easiest to use a potato ricer or a potato masher. If you don't have either, mash them on a plate using a big fork.

• Add the milk and butter and stir.

• Heat them in a pan on the stove until they just start to bubble gently. Stir all the time, so they don't stick to the bottom of the pan. If you want runnier mashed potatoes, add some more milk. Salt to taste.

• Take the pan off the heat and stir in some chopped parsley. Serve immediately. Chives are also good with mashed potatoes, but stir them in just before you're ready to eat or the chives will give the potatoes a sour taste. I know, because I made that mistake once.

Potato Sandwich

Have you ever tried putting cold sliced boiled potatoes on an open-faced sandwich, maybe with some chopped chives or dill on top?

Potato Salad

Leftover cooked potatoes can be used in a salad. Peel them and cut them in small pieces, or slice them and then put them in vinaigrette or yogurt dressing (the recipes are on page 26).

You can also add other good things to the salad: dill, leeks, chives, pickles, or pickled beets, all finely chopped. Capers are tiny green buds from caper bushes, pickled in salt and vinegar. I think they're good in potato salad, but Arthur thinks they're too strong.

Creamed Potatoes

Did you know you can cook potatoes in milk? They're really good, too! You have to peel the potatoes first and cut them up into small pieces. You'll need about 1/3 cup of milk for 3 medium-size potatoes.

• In a pot heat the milk to the boiling point. Keep an eye on it, because milk boils over with no warning!

• Add the cut-up potatoes and a little salt. Turn down the heat when the milk starts boiling again, so it won't burn. Put a lid on the pot and let the potatoes cook *slowly*. They should be soft after about 15 minutes.

• When the potatoes are done, stir in a handful of cut dill. Serve with – well, you'll have to decide that yourself!

creamed, boiled, baked ...

Fried Potatoes

Usually you just cut *cooked* potatoes into small pieces and fry them. If the skins are thin, you can leave them on. You can also fry raw potatoes. Of course, that takes a little longer. Fry them on *low* heat, using vegetable oil or as little butter as possible, since potatoes soak it up and fat is not all that good for you.

Potato Soup

Arthur's best soup. We make it without bouillon cubes (other cookbooks use bouillon cubes) because we think the soup is better and tastes more like potatoes without bouillon.

SOUP FOR TWO:

1 leek
2 large potatoes
1 tbsp. butter
$1^{2}/_{3}$ cups water (to begin with)
$1/_{2}$ cup water (later)
$1/_{2}$ tsp. salt
A little pepper
$1/_{2}$ cup milk
Chopped chives or parsley

HERE'S WHAT YOU DO:

• Rinse the leek *well* (make a cut lengthwise, so you can get at the inside). Cut the leek into thin slices (rings).
• Peel the raw potatoes and cut them into small pieces (don't grate them – the soup won't be as good).

• Carefully melt the butter in a pot. When it stops sputtering, add the sliced leek. Stir until the leek is soft, but don't let it burn, *whatever you do*. I did that once, and I had to throw everything out and start all over again.
• Add $1^{2}/_{3}$ cups water, heating it until it boils. Add the potatoes, salt, and pepper. Now the soup should cook *slowly* for 20 minutes, so it's best to turn the heat down to low. At the end of the cooking time, you can whip the potatoes with a beater. The soup should be smooth and somewhat thick.
• Now add another $1/_{2}$ cup water and $1/_{2}$ cup milk. Turn up the heat. Just before the soup starts to boil, take it off the stove.
• Serve it in bowls with chopped chives or parsley sprinkled over the top. Eat it right away with a cheese sandwich, a glass of milk, and maybe a tomato, too.

Baked Potatoes

• Heat the oven to 425°F. Line a baking pan with aluminum foil (so you won't have to wash it later).
• Wash the potatoes and cut them in half lengthwise. Put the halves on the foil.
• Brush the tops with olive or other vegetable oil and sprinkle them with some salt and caraway seeds if you like those.
• Put the pan in the oven. After a half hour, I usually ask a grownup to check to see if they're done (it's easy to burn yourself). When the potatoes feel soft they are ready.
• Try some other seasonings, too. Baked potatoes are good with all kinds of meat.

What all of me needs

You can't live on just potatoes. Well, actually you can, but it would be much too boring. It's a good thing there are other kinds of food that are good for you. Arthur and I read about them in a book we borrowed from the library.

The body is made up of small cells (just like the potato!). Bones, muscles, skin, hair, nails, everything is made up of cells, tiny rooms all close together.

One amazing thing we read was: The body (and the cells) are mostly water. More than half of our body is water!

About half the food we eat is also only water. The rest is a combination of these things:

• PROTEIN This is so important that without it there would be no life at all. Protein is needed as a fuel for the body and as building blocks for the cells. Without cells there would be no people, no animals, no plants.

Plants can make their own protein from material in water, soil, and air. That's something animals and people can't do. But we *must* have protein, so we get it by eating plants, or by eating animals that have eaten plants.

Foods that are especially rich in protein, such as *fish, poultry, meat, eggs, milk,* and *cheese,* all come from animals. Other high-protein foods such as *beans, flour, grain, nuts,* and *certain vegetables* come from plants.

• FAT The body also needs fat as a fuel in order to work, play, and keep warm. Foods especially rich in fat are *margarine, oil, butter,* and *cream* (and *whipped cream!*).

• CARBOHYDRATES These are also fuels. There are several different kinds of carbohydrates. Some taste sweet. Ordinary sugar (from sugarcane or sugar beets) is found in *soft drinks* and *candy.* This kind of sugar is not very good for your body. But the sugar in fruit, honey, and milk has some food value.

Another carbohydrate is starch. It's found in *cereals, pasta, potatoes,* and *vegetables.*

Plant fibers are also carbohydrates. They are supports found in the cell walls of plants, instead of the bones we humans have. (Without bones I bet we'd all be lying in piles on the ground!) We can't digest fiber, though, so what is it good for? Well, it gives our digestive system a workout, and that's *really* important. (Arthur will explain more about that on page 21.)

• VITAMINS The body doesn't use these so much for fuel but more like . . . well, like tools maybe, to get the building blocks and the fuel to work. Vitamins are so small that they are invisible.

Foods that are especially rich in vitamins are *fruits, vegetables, potatoes* and other *root vegetables, milk, meat, fish,* and *cheese.*

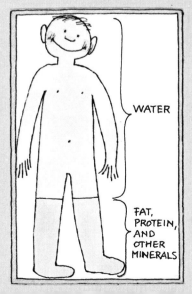

WATER

FAT, PROTEIN, AND OTHER MINERALS

• MINERALS We have to have these in our diet, too, if we want to stay healthy. There are some minerals that we need so little of they are called *trace elements.* Copper and zinc are two of these. We need more of other minerals, such as iron (for our blood) and calcium (for bones and teeth). *Milk* and *cheese* are especially rich in calcium. *Liver, whole grains,* and *leafy green vegetables* (like spinach) are high in iron.

• FOOD GROUPS WHEEL is what the above circle is called. Foods are divided into seven groups.

Go easy on the oil, butter, and margarine group. You should eat as little fat as possible, since you will still get enough of it from other foods, like the ones in the milk, cheese, and yogurt group. (And those foods also have lots of protein, vitamins, and minerals.)

The bread, flour, and cereal group also gives us protein, as well as vitamins, minerals, and the very important fiber. Potatoes also provide fiber and vitamins.

We should eat a lot of fresh fruits and vegetables every day. That way we'll get the fiber, vitamins, and minerals we need.

The most protein is found in the meat, poultry, fish, and egg group. But meat is an expensive food, and too much meat isn't healthy anyway. People who eat no meat or fish are called *vegetarians*. They get their protein from foods in the milk group, beans, nuts, and breads.

What a cow can do

"Imagine being able to make *milk* out of *grass*," I said. "Cows can do that. Isn't *that* fantastic!"

"But cows can't make *all* the milk," said Arthur. "Isn't some of it made in factories?"

"No," said Stella. "Cows really do make all the milk. No factory can do it."

"But how do cows *do it*, then?" I asked.

"They use their four stomachs," said Stella. "I remember learning that in school."

"Four stomachs!" said Arthur. "Wow!"

"When a cow eats grass, she doesn't chew it up very well," said Stella. "Then when she swallows, the big mouthfuls land in two stomachs that start to digest the food.

"A little while later, the cow spits up a mouthful at a time, back into her mouth, where she chews it again. This is called chewing her cud.

"When she swallows the next time, the food ends up in two new stomachs.

"When all four stomachs have finished their work, the food (nourishment) moves on into the intestine. From there the blood sucks it up and carries it around the body.

"Much of the nourishment goes to the mam-mary glands, which make the milk. The grass that the cow ate has now been turned into quali-ty protein.

"What does a cow need all that milk for? Well, it's for her calves, of course; just the way babies drink milk from their mother's breasts.

"A long, long time ago, all cows were wild animals. Then cows had milk in their udders only when they had a newborn calf. But when people started to catch wild cows and tame them, they kept on milking the cows after the calves had stopped nursing. That way they fooled the cows into making more milk. A cow still has to have a calf every year if she is going to continue making milk."

Stella also told us that you have to be nice to a cow when you milk her. Otherwise, she may not let down her milk. She likes to have some-thing special to eat and to have her udder and teats cleaned first, and she likes to be milked by someone she knows. Nowadays, most milking is done by machine. A tube with a suction cup is attached to each teat. That way one person can milk three or four cows at the same time.

We get almost a third of our protein from

NOW SOMETHING'S HAPPENING!

cow's milk, and almost a third of our fat, too. Plus a large part of the vitamins and minerals that we need.

"So cows must really be our best friends," said Arthur.

Hello.
How much milk does she give?

Since Stella didn't know how much milk a cow could give in one day, we called the local dairy and asked.

"A normal cow can produce an average of about five gallons a day, more after she calves, and nothing at all just before," said the man who answered the phone. That would be about 1,300 gallons a year! Many cows produce even more.

SOME OF THE THINGS WE CAN GET FROM ONE COW'S MILK

WHOLE MILK
SKIM MILK
BUTTERMILK
KEFIR
YOGURT
WHIPPING CREAM
HALF-AND-HALF
SOUR CREAM
BUTTER
CHEESE
COTTAGE CHEESE
POWDERED MILK
ICE CREAM

"A cow needs about 12 tons of food and 5,000 gallons of water a year to do her job," the man from the dairy told us.

"Oh," we said. "Thanks for the information."

We make butter

"I have some whipping cream," said Stella, "so we can try to make butter today."

We used an egg beater to beat the cream. First it turned into whipped cream – I mean really thick whipped cream. But we kept on going.

Suddenly the cream got grainy, and then it got all lumpy. And at the same time, some of it turned into a thin, watery milk.

"That's called buttermilk," said Stella, "and the other stuff is called butter!"

We poured off the buttermilk and put the butter in a little jar. From one cup of whipping cream we got about half a cup of butter. We salted the butter and stirred it. Then we each made ourselves a sandwich with homemade butter.

Champion Cow Bella

Here is Bella. She is sixteen years old and has had thirteen calves. She gives 2,148 gallons of milk a year! That's an average of about 31 quarts a day for those months of the year when she gives milk! Normal cows usually give an average of about 20 quarts a day, or about 1,300 gallons a year. So you see what a champion Bella is!

Snack à la Bella

Most of this snack is provided by Bella (or some other cow).
- Butter a cracker or a piece of bread.
- Put a good-size piece of cheese on top.
- Pour a big glass of milk.
- Serve with a tomato (or slice the tomato and put it on top of the cheese).

Cranberry Yogurt

This is a way to make ordinary plain yogurt extra good. It will be creamy pink. Here's what you do for one serving:

Beat 1 cup of yogurt with 2 tbsp. of cranberry preserves.

Pour it into a bowl and add an extra dab of cranberry.

Linnea's Cheese

A girl we know named Linnea showed us how to make this soft cheese spread:

- Set a coffee filter holder over a jar. Put in a paper coffee filter.
- Pour in a cup of commercial sour cream or yogurt.
- Wait 24 hours. The sour cream has now separated. The part still up in the filter is thick; it has become cheese. Down in the jar is a transparent liquid called whey. (Remember little Miss Muffet?)
- From 1 cup of sour cream we got $1/2$ cup of cheese.
- The cheese can be seasoned, too. We've tried different seasonings: $1/2$ tsp. herbs (try different combinations of fresh or dried basil, thyme, dill, or oregano) or $1/2$ tsp. ground paprika and some salt and chopped watercress. Anyone who likes garlic (me!) can use that, too (use a little bit of fresh, very finely chopped garlic). We also tried caraway seeds, but Arthur didn't like that.

thank cows for

Elvira's Ice Cream

Stella's friend Elvira makes ice cream for us sometimes. This ice cream is only for special occasions, because whipped cream and sugar aren't good for you. The recipe makes a giant portion which is really big enough for two.

HERE'S WHAT YOU NEED:

1 tbsp. confectioners' sugar
¹/₈ tsp. vanilla
1 egg yolk
6 tbsp. whipping cream

HERE'S WHAT YOU DO:

• Put the confectioners' sugar, vanilla, and egg yolk in a small mixing bowl. Beat until the mixture is thick and light yellow.
• Whip the cream in another bowl. Add it to the other mixture, stirring only enough to mix.
• Pour the ice cream mixture into a bowl or plastic container that will fit in the freezer. Cover. In my freezer it took 4 hours for the ice cream to harden, but it can take longer.

   If you use real vanilla and a little more sugar, it will taste even better. Real vanilla is more expensive than vanilla flavoring. Stella says that real vanilla grows on the island of Madagascar, off the coast of Africa. It's made from the seedpods of climbing orchids.

Exotic Milk Drinks

We like to whip up different milk drinks. We use a hand mixer and a bowl for this (you can also use a blender). You can use whole milk, but we think the drinks get even frothier with skim milk. The milk looks exotic when we pour it into tall glasses. Each recipe makes one tall drink, except for the orange milk recipe, which makes two (because of the egg yolk).

HERE'S WHAT YOU NEED:

²/₃ cup skim milk
¹/₂ cup raspberries (fresh or frozen)
1 tsp. sugar
or:
²/₃ cup skim milk
3 tbsp. cranberry sauce (or jam)
or:
²/₃ cup skim milk
Juice of 1 orange
1 egg yolk

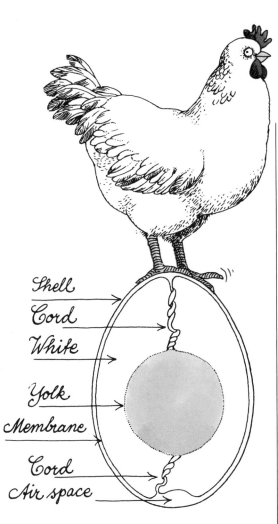

Shell
Cord
White

Yolk
Membrane

Cord
Air space

Thank heaven

Some hen history

A long, long time ago, hens were wild jungle fowl. They lived in India and other places in Asia. At that time hens didn't lay anywhere near as many eggs as they do today. They would lay eggs only a few times a year after mating with a rooster.

A hen sat on her eggs in a nest. After a while they hatched and out came the chicks, which grew up to be new hens and roosters.

Just as they did with cows, people tamed hens. And in the thousands of years that followed, people changed the hen and her habits.

• Nowadays we let certain hens do *nothing* but lay eggs to be eaten (laying hens).

• Certain hens lay *only* fertilized eggs (breeding hens).

• And certain hens do *nothing* but grow, to be eaten later (broilers). Laying hens are allowed to live about a year, and then they are killed and used for food. Breeding hens get to live for two years, but broilers are killed when they're between three and five months old.

"Just think, every egg that we eat has been laid by a hen," I said.

"I don't want to think about what *part* of the hen it came out of," said Arthur.

"Oh, that doesn't matter," I said. "You don't eat the shell, you know."

"Eggs are good food," said Stella. "They contain protein and vitamins and iron. Especially the yolk."

"Can there be chickens in the eggs that you buy?" asked Arthur.

"No," said Stella. "Most eggs are laid by hens who have never even met a rooster. A rooster has to mate with a hen if there are going to be any chickens in the eggs."

"Can hens lay eggs anyway, even when they haven't mated?" I asked.

"Yes, they can," said Stella. "A good hen can lay an egg nearly every day."

SOME MISERABLE HENS ON A FACTORY FARM...

for little hens

Some hens you should feel sorry for

A lot of people keep their hens in crowded cages because it is cheaper to feed and take care of hens in this way. There are often ten thousand caged hens in a single building. You could call it a hen factory. Hens have been known to rub off their feathers on the cages. Sometimes they start pecking and plucking each other's feathers just because they're so uncomfortable.

Some chicken farmers cut off the ends of the animals' beaks so they won't be able to peck at one another. Roosters' combs have even been cut off, so they won't be able to recognize each other, since roosters peck each other more often than hens do.

By the time they're killed, broilers might have lost all their feathers.

"Are they *allowed* to do that?" I asked. "There should be a law against it! When I grow up I'm going to work for such a law, even if it means eggs will cost more because hens are being treated better."

The art of cooking an egg

Hard-boiling an egg is easy, but cooking an egg so that the yolk is runny while the white is firm – that's an art!

PERFECT !!!

HERE'S WHAT YOU DO:
- Boil some water in a pot.
- Carefully put the egg in the boiling water, with the help of a spoon so it won't crack.
- Start timing it now. A medium-size egg directly from the refrigerator should take 5 minutes; 4 minutes if it's at room temperature.
- When the time is up, take the pan off the stove (turn it off) and rinse the egg in cold water a little while. That way it will stop cooking and be easier to peel (according to some people).
- Hard-boiled eggs take 10–12 minutes.

How does an egg cook?

When an egg gets warm, its protein hardens, starting with the white, which is closer to the outside. At 140 degrees it's like jelly, and at 160 degrees it's really firm. We say that it has *coagulated*.

The yolk coagulates, too, but it takes 5 to 6 minutes for the heat to get through the white. After 7 to 10 minutes the egg has reached 160 degrees all the way through. Then the yolk is also hard. The egg is hard-boiled.

THIS IS THE WAY ALL HENS SHOULD LIVE

17

Eggs aren't bad at all

I fry an egg

Now I've got my own *small* iron frying pan. It's not as heavy as the big ones. It's especially good if you want to fry only *one* egg.

I crack an egg on the edge of a cup. Carefully, I let the yolk and the white slide down into the cup.

I heat the frying pan, and put in some butter – just a little. Butter is mostly fat, of course, but there are some protein and water in it, too. When the butter melts in the pan, it starts sputtering. When it stops sputtering, that means that the water has cooked away. Now it's time to let the egg slide out of the cup down into the frying pan. Don't wait until the butter turns brown (that means the protein in the butter has burned). Burned butter doesn't taste good, and it isn't good for you. It would be better to pour it out and start over again.

The egg white coagulates and turns white in the frying pan almost immediately. I turn down the heat.

When all the egg white is white, the egg is done. I pick it up carefully with a spatula and lift it onto my plate.

Arthur thinks runny yolks are disgusting, so he usually turns his eggs over and cooks them on the other side, too. That's called over easy.

Mushroom-in-the-Woods

This is a dish for two people (who like spinach).

HERE'S WHAT YOU NEED:
2 eggs
10-oz. package frozen spinach
1 tomato
Some mayonnaise

HERE'S WHAT YOU DO:
• Hard-boil the eggs (10 minutes).
• Heat the spinach in a pan (on low heat). It takes a while to thaw. Peel the eggs while you wait. Slice off the rounded ends of the eggs, so they can sit upright without rolling over.
• Arrange the spinach on two plates. (It's nicer if the plates are warm. You can heat them up first by putting them in warm water for a few minutes.)
• Place the eggs, cut end down, in the spinach.
• Cut a tomato in half for the 2 mushroom caps. Put the halves carefully on top of the eggs.
• Decorate the mushrooms with white polka dots of mayonnaise. (Real mushrooms that look like this are poisonous. *Don't ever eat them.* But you probably already knew that.)

Omelets are easy

They are especially easy to make in my *small* frying pan. Big omelets almost always fall apart when I make them.

HERE'S WHAT YOU NEED TO MAKE MY OMELET:

1 egg
1 tsp. cold water
Salt and pepper
1 tsp. butter for frying

HERE'S WHAT YOU DO:

• Crack the egg against the edge of a big cup. Pour the yolk and the white into the cup.
• Add the water, salt and pepper.
• Beat with a fork until everything is well mixed, but not any longer.
• Heat the butter in a small frying pan. When the butter stops sputtering, it's time to add the egg mixture. Turn down the heat. Stir a little with a fork.
• The omelet is ready when it's firm around the edges, but it can still be a little soft and glossy in the middle.
• Fold the omelet in half and slide it over to your plate. You can make a mushroom omelet by putting sliced mushrooms in the middle. (I cook them first in butter.) Chopped parsley is also good in an omelet.

Marble Eggs

Wrap a raw egg in onion skins from a red or yellow onion. Cover the egg with aluminum foil to keep the skins in place. Hard-boil the egg the usual way. Take off the foil and the skins and you'll see that the egg looks as if it's made of marble. Yellow and red skins make different colors, but I'm not saying which ones.

Where does all the food go?

We eat and eat and eat, but where does all that food go? Arthur and I went back to the library and looked it up. It was complicated, so Stella had to help us. This is how it works:

• For the body to make use of a ham sandwich, for example, it needs to digest it first. That means it must break it down into tiny, tiny pieces, and then break it down chemically into even smaller parts called *nutrients* (fat, protein, carbohydrates – you remember from page 10).

• As soon as the ham sandwich is in your mouth, your body starts working. First, your *teeth* cut and grind the sandwich into small pieces. Your *tongue* is the big muscle that stirs it all around, so everything will get chewed. At this point, your *saliva* (spit) has already started to break down the food chemically. It also soaks the dry bread so that it can be easily swallowed.

"Wow!" said Arthur. "It says here that the saliva glands produce $1\frac{1}{2}$ quarts of saliva every twenty-four hours. Imagine that, $1\frac{1}{2}$ quarts of spit!"

• When we decide to swallow, the food slides down through the *esophagus* (food canal). After that everything happens automatically. Different muscles continue to push the ham sandwich down into the *stomach,* whether we want them to or not.

• The stomach is an expandable sack. An adult stomach can hold from 1 to $1\frac{1}{2}$ quarts. As soon as we see the ham sandwich, our brain sends signals to our stomach to start making *gastric juice.* Gastric juice (like saliva) contains something called *enzymes,* which are strong chemical substances that break down food (digest it). The ham sandwich mixed with gastric juice becomes a sort of very watery oatmeal.

The part that takes the longest time to break down is the butter (fat). The ham (protein) also takes a long time. But the carbohydrates in the bread are taken care of in a couple of hours. If there had been jam on the bread, the sugar in the jam would have gone almost right through the stomach, which doesn't have to work on it. That's why you feel fuller longer after eating

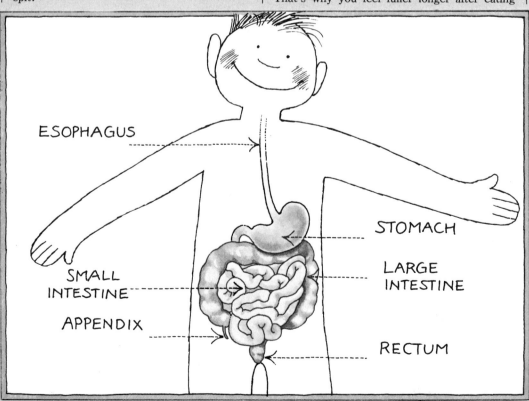

ESOPHAGUS

STOMACH

LARGE INTESTINE

SMALL INTESTINE

APPENDIX

RECTUM

GUESS WHAT IS 20 FEET LONG...

... AND FUZZY INSIDE!

food that is high in fat and protein, and hungry again soon after eating candy or drinking sodas, which contain so much sugar.

"What makes your stomach growl?" I asked.

"Maybe it says in the book," said Stella.

• The stomach works as a container, we read. It releases small portions at a time into the *small intestine.* There *intestinal juices* (made with new enzymes) make the food even mushier. No one could ever guess that all that mush was once a ham sandwich.

"Twenty feet!" said Arthur. "The small intestine is about twenty feet long! It lies like a tangled-up tube under the stomach."

"And all fuzzy inside!" I said. It looked like velvet. The finger-like points which line the small intestine are called *intestinal villi.* They suck up the nourishment and pass it on to the blood, which carries it all through the body.

"Look at that wormy thing hanging under the *large intestine,*" said Arthur. "What's that for?"

"Nothing, as far as I know," said Stella. "The *appendix* doesn't go anywhere. But it can swell up and become very painful, and then it has to be taken out."

When all the nourishment has been sucked up through the small intestine, there is only indigestible bread fiber, water, and waste left. That moves on into the large intestine. Some of the water is sucked up and disappears through the intestinal wall. That makes the mush firmer again, sometimes even rather hard. It collects in the lower part of the large intestine, and that's when we feel the need to go to the bathroom.

Now we finally get to decide by ourselves again. We can decide to empty the intestine by having a bowel movement. The end of the large intestine is called the *rectum.* There are strong muscles there that can squeeze out the waste, and then close the hole (*anus*) afterward.

"Well," said Stella, "now we know something about what our bodies do with food."

"That's right," I said. "But we still never found out what makes our stomachs growl."

Eat more fiber!

Arthur showed us a newspaper clipping.

"Want to hear something *interesting*? Listen to this," said Arthur. "In Africa, people have bowel movements five times as often as we do here in the Western world."

"The Western world – that includes North America and Europe," said Stella.

"And guess why," said Arthur. "It's because they eat more *fiber* than we do. We think it's better to eat easy-to-chew food, but that's wrong!"

"Why is fiber so good, then?" I asked.

"It says here that fiber makes the stomach and intestines exercise, and if they don't exercise we get sick," said Arthur.

"That's right," said Stella. "Since we started eating food low in fiber, we've been getting a lot of new diseases that they don't have in countries where they eat a lot of fiber."

"But what if that's only because they're different from us," I said.

"No way," said Arthur. "Because if those people start eating Western food, they get these diseases, too, after a few years. It says so right here."

We also read that fiber sucks up a lot of water. That means that body waste becomes softer and moves easier and faster through the large intestine. That's fine, because it's not good for you to carry waste around for a week at a time. People who eat lots of fiber get rid of the waste after only one or two days.

WAYS TO GET MORE FIBER

• Eat whole-grain bread and crackers instead of white bread.

• Use whole-grain flours (such as whole-wheat, stone-ground rye, and oat flours) for baking and cooking hot cereal.

• Bran has a high fiber content. Buy some (it's cheap) and try it on your cereal.

• Eat more foods from the plant kingdom: peas, beans, vegetables, root vegetables, fruits, and berries instead of fatty hot dogs and sandwich spreads.

• Eat as little sugar and fat as possible, because they have no fiber at all.

Hurrah for the plant kingdom!

My favorite picture is of a man who's made up entirely of fruit and vegetables. It's called *The Gardener*. I have a postcard of it on my wall. That's because I'm crazy about vegetables.

There is *not* much protein or fat in many vegetables. They are mostly water and carbohydrates.

Well then, what's the point of eating vegetables, you may wonder. First of all, they taste so good (most of them anyway), and second, they have so many important vitamins and minerals. And most of their carbohydrates are the kind that are high in fiber and good for your body. That's why you should eat vegetables every day. It's lucky they taste so good!

Fresh vegetables taste best and are the best for you, but frozen ones are almost as good.

THE GARDENER PAINTED BY GIUSEPPE ARCHIMBOLDO IN THE 16TH CENTURY

Canned vegetables are not as good. Both the taste and the amount of vitamins suffer in the canning process.

Whether you plan to eat vegetables raw or cooked, you have to wash them well in cold water first. This is because vegetables (and fruit) can have soil, dirt, or pesticides left on them that can be dangerous for your body.

This is how I cook vegetables

I always get the water boiling *before* putting in the vegetables, so that the vitamins have a better chance of surviving. I use only enough water to just cover the vegetables. For every pint of water you need $\frac{1}{2}$ tsp. salt. Then I let the water boil slowly, not bubble over, with a lid. When I can prick the vegetables easily with a fork or knife, they are done. They should be crisp, not mushy. *Don't* cook them any longer. Throw away the water and eat the vegetables immediately.

Grass Sandwich

I cut some dill, parsley, watercress or garden cress, and chives onto a plate. Then I butter a piece of bread and dip it into the cut herbs. They stick to the bread and make a grass sandwich.

Cress and chives grow in my kitchen window. *Garden cress* I start from seed on a piece of damp cotton placed on a plate. (The package tells you how to do it.) I buy the *chives* in little containers. They should be replanted in real pots and cut often.

MY FAVORITES

AVOCADOS I CUT IN HALF AND EAT WITH A SPOON, WITH SALAD DRESSING IN THE HOLE WHERE THE PIT WAS (I CAN PLANT THE PIT IN A POT LATER).

BRUSSELS SPROUTS LOOK LIKE LITTLE DOLL CABBAGES. I COOK THEM 10 TO 15 MINUTES (THE CABBAGES, NOT THE DOLLS). ARTHUR THINKS THEY TASTE BITTER.

CUCUMBERS ARE ALWAYS GOOD!

CARROTS I EAT RAW, OR COOKED, OR FRIED WITH ROSEMARY OR THYME (HERBS).

ARTICHOKES ARE BIG THISTLES. I COOK THEM 30 TO 45 MINUTES, LET THEM DRAIN, SQUEEZE SOME LEMON OVER THEM, AND THEN EAT THE SOFT PART OF EACH PETAL WITH BUTTER. INSIDE ALL THE PETALS IS THE HAIRY CHOKE, WHICH I CUT AWAY. HURRAH! THE BEST PART IS LEFT: THE HEART.

LEEKS I EAT RAW IN SALADS OR COOK LIKE THE CAULI-FLOWER ON PAGE 42.

RADISHES THE WAY STELLA HAD THEM WHEN SHE WAS LITTLE: I CUT AN X ON THE TOP AND SQUEEZE IN A DAB OF BUTTER —RADISH ICE CREAM.

BEETS (FRESH): I CUT OFF THE LEAVES (NOT THE STEMS), RINSE, COOK FOR 20 MINUTES, PEEL, AND EAT WITH BUTTER AND SALT. THERE IS A RECIPE FOR BEET SOUP ON PAGE 41.

RINSE EVERY MORNING AND EVENING

FIRST DAY

SECOND DAY

THIRD DAY

There's a girl named Linnea who lives in my building. She gave me two little bags, one with tiny brown seeds called *alfalfa* seeds and one with bigger green *mung beans.*

"You want to see some magic?" said Linnea. "It will take a few days, though."

I wanted to.

"Then I'll show you how to grow sprouts," said Linnea. "Do you have two glass jars?"

"No, bigger than that. There has to be room for at least a quart."

We poured $\frac{1}{4}$ cup alfalfa seeds in one jar and $\frac{1}{4}$ cup mung beans in the other. Linnea had two pieces of cheesecloth that we fastened over the jars with rubber bands.

Then we filled the jars with lukewarm water. "They have to soak the first night," said Linnea.

"When does the magic part start?" I asked.

"Maybe tomorrow night," said Linnea. "Tomorrow morning you should pour off the water. You can use it for watering your plants, because it's full of things that are good for them. Then you should put fresh water in the jars, and pour it out again. Put the jars upside down in the dish drainer to get rid of all the water. Then put the jars in a dark cupboard. It can't be some place cold, or it will take too long. You have to rinse the jars twice a day, morning and night, and let all the water drain off."

"It sounds complicated," I said.

"It may *sound* complicated," said Linnea, "but it's really very *simple.*"

I did just what Linnea had said. The next night I could see small white spots or points on some of the seeds and beans.

But by the *next* day the magic had really started. Tiny white tails were sticking out of the seeds and beans. The jar was fuller!

By the third day the sprouts had grown so much that there was at least five times as much in the mung bean jar compared to the first day! Maybe even more than that in the alfalfa jar.

By the fourth day the jar was nearly full! The green shells had started to fall off the mung beans.

"Of course, it's not really magic," said Linnea. "Seeds sprout when they get water and heat. Alfalfa and mung beans sprout even more than other seeds. Tomorrow you should put the jars in the light after you rinse them."

Guess what happened then? Well, after a few hours the sprouts turned green!

"The green is *chlorophyll,*" said Linnea. "Small green particles that help the plant make its food from air and water. Since chlorophyll is run on solar energy, the sprouts had to come out into the light before they could become green."

Finally we were able to taste the sprouts. They were nice and crunchy when we bit into them. They tasted different, but both kinds were *good*!

"They can keep for up to a week in the refrigerator," said Linnea. "They stop growing, which is fine, since they're at their best right now."

Since then I've sprouted many seeds and beans. And there are lots of ways to use sprouts.

vegetables

ALFALFA SEEDS

MUNG BEANS

FOURTH DAY

FIFTH DAY

Here's how I use my sprouts:

1. On sandwiches. Over cheese spread. Or like this: First butter a slice of whole-grain bread. Then spread a *little* horseradish sauce on top. Add a thin slice of corned beef, and on top of that a tangle of sprouts! But don't put too much horseradish on or your nostrils will sting (clears your head, is what grownups said about horseradish when Stella was young).
2. In salads. Try them with lettuce and slices of a vegetable called *fennel.* Or just use sliced tomatoes. There is a recipe for salad dressing on the next page.
3. In soups. But put them in at the last minute, just before the soup is ready to be served.

IMPORTANT!

• Don't forget to let the water drain off the sprouts after each rinsing. Otherwise they can get moldy and you'll have to throw them all out.

• Always take out the mung beans that haven't sprouted. They're as hard as rocks if you bite into one.

• Don't think that all seeds and beans can be sprouted. Some of them don't taste good, and some are even poisonous when they sprout. Lentils are good, and alfalfa and mung beans are *extra nutritious* when they're sprouting because they make a lot of vitamins just then, not to mention all the protein and fiber they have (and the fact that they taste good). The Chinese discovered all of that thousands of years ago.

"Look at my taste buds!"

That's what Arthur was shouting when I went up to Stella's one day.

"Let's see," I said. "I don't see any buds, just your old tongue."

"I was just kidding," said Arthur. "Taste buds are so small you can't even see them with a magnifying glass. But you see those little bumps that look like the fuzz on a beach towel?"

"Yeah, I see them," I said.

"Every one of those bumps has about 100 taste buds. There are about 10,000 of them altogether."

"No wonder there are so many different tastes," I said.

"*Actually,* there are only four tastes," said Stella. "Sweet, salty, sour, and bitter."

"What about all those other tastes?" I said. "Vanilla and strawberry and garlic and . . ."

"Those are all smells (aromas) that our noses sense," said Stella. "Even if we *think* we're tasting them in our mouth, we're not. Close your eyes and hold your nose. Now let's see if you can tell what you're eating if you don't know ahead of time."

Two salad dressings

1. VINAIGRETTE is the most common salad dressing. You make it by mixing 1 tbsp. vinegar with 4 tbsp. olive oil. Then you add salt and pepper, garlic (for those who like it), or a pinch of dried herbs (try different mixtures of basil, thyme, or oregano).

2. YOGURT DRESSING is a little thicker and creamier. It's really good if you add 1 tbsp. mayonnaise to $\frac{1}{3}$ cup plain yogurt (or kefir). Add a little milk if you want it thinner. Season with salt and pepper and *curry powder,* if you wish. Garlic and *tarragon* are other good seasonings for yogurt dressing.

+ a beautiful salad

I think it's fun to arrange food attractively on a plate, the way you see below:

● Lettuce ● canned corn ● crisp bacon bits (with the fat drained off onto paper towels) ● cauliflower (broken into flowerets, then sliced crosswise like little trees) ● leek rings (cleaned) ● shrimp (if you have some) ● a radish in the middle

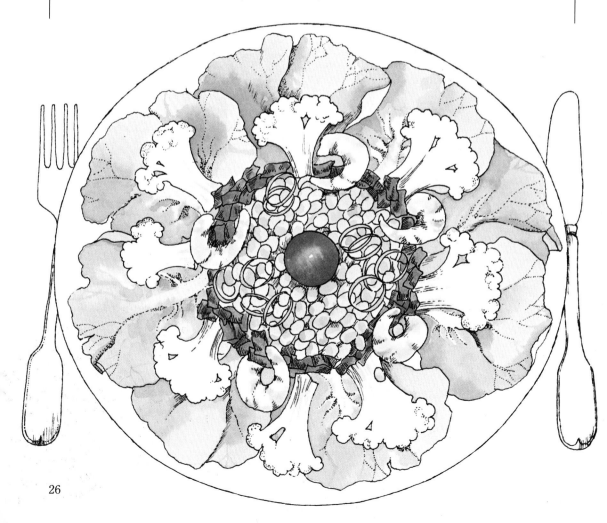

My cook's apron

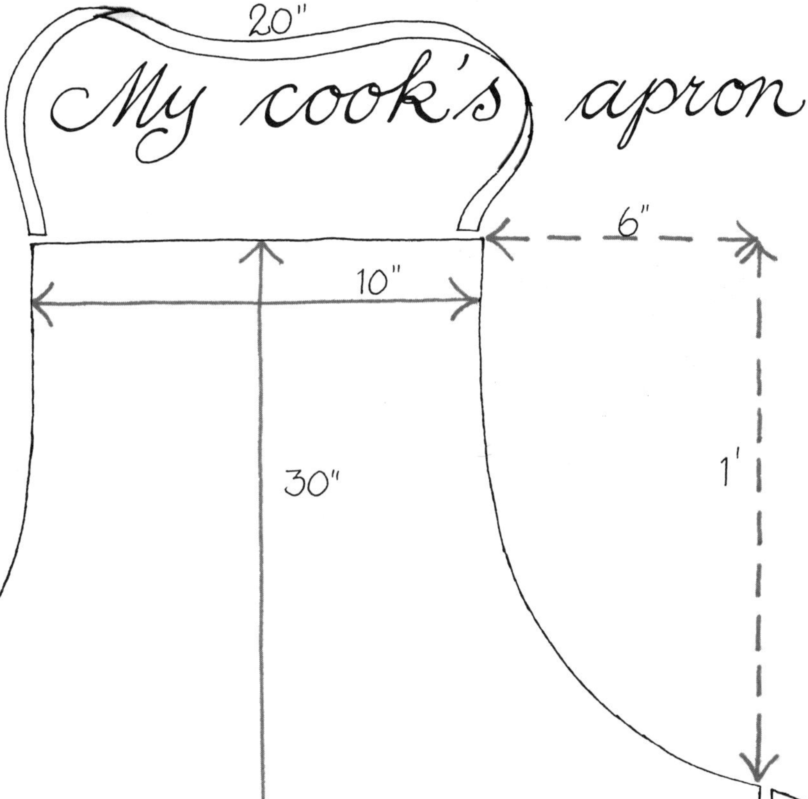

20"

6"

10"

30"

1'

3'4" (left side)

3'4" (right side)

22"

Tomorrow I'm going to bake, so I made myself an apron. Like this:

- I found an old sheet. I cut out a piece about 22 inches wide and 30 inches long from the least worn-out end.

- An apron is supposed to be narrower at the top, so I laid it out on the floor and marked the way I would cut it. Here are the measurements. To get the curved lines nice and even, I traced around the edge of a big pizza pan.

- I cut the apron out and tried it on for size. It seemed fine.

- Then I zigzag stitched all around the edges on the sewing machine. (You can sew it by hand, but it takes a lot longer!)

- Next I sewed a $1/4$-inch hem all the way around, using the straight stitch on the machine.

- Now only the strings were left. I used white cotton twill tape. I pinned one end to the corner of the top part of the apron. Then I tried it on to see how long the tape should be to go around my neck. I marked it with a pin and cut the twill tape. It was about 20 inches long.

- I turned under the end of the twill tape (about $1/2$ inch) and pinned it to the apron corner. Then I carefully machine-stitched it in place with an X in the center.

I SEWED THE STRINGS ON SECURELY

THE BACK

- I wanted the apron strings to be long enough to tie in front. That took about 3 feet for each string. I sewed them on the same way to the apron (with an X in the center). Then I tied a little knot in the end of each string so it wouldn't unravel.

- I had planned to make pockets, but I ran out of steam. Maybe next time.

$\mathscr{I}$ bake my

"Be nice to the yeast," said Stella. "It's alive."

"Living yeast!" I said. "Are we going to have *living yeast* in our bread dough?"

"We certainly are," said Stella. "The living cells in the yeast are what make the dough rise. Otherwise, the bread would be heavy, flat, and boring. But right now the yeast is still asleep in the packet.

"Let's make a small batch. We'll use just one packet of dry yeast."

Stella measured out a cup of warm water.

"Now we'll wake up the yeast,"

she said. "But it's very *important* that the water is not *too* warm. It should be about 110 to 115 degrees. Feel it with your finger. It should feel slightly warm, but absolutely not hot, a little warmer than you are yourself."

After I'd tested the water temperature, I poured a little water into a bowl and added the yeast and $\frac{1}{4}$ tsp. sugar. Then I mixed everything together with a wooden spoon until the yeast was dissolved. After that, I poured in the rest of the water and added $\frac{1}{2}$ tsp. salt.

I measured out $2\frac{1}{2}$ cups of flour and added it to the water, sugar, salt, and yeast, stirring in a little at a time. The dough got thicker and thicker. Actually, I didn't use all the flour, but saved about $\frac{1}{4}$ cup for later.

When the dough was all nice and evenly mixed and smooth on the outside, we put the bowl next to the stove and covered it with a clean dish towel.

"Now it's going to rise," said Stella. "That will take about a half hour."

When we looked after a half hour, the dough had risen all the way up to the dish towel.

"Just like magic!"

I said. "How could it grow like that?"

Stella didn't know exactly, so we looked it up in her biggest cookbook. It said that when you mix flour with water, you get a dough with lots of "dough threads" in it. And when we wake up the yeast by getting it warm and wet, it starts making small gas bubbles (carbon dioxide) among the threads. The gas bubbles make the dough swell and sort of puff up, and that's why the bread becomes light and porous.

Stella spread out the flour we had saved on the countertop next to the stove. Then she took out the dough (it stuck to the bowl with all of its threads). "Now you have to knead it," said Stella. "Push and turn the dough with the palms of your hands. Work it quickly and easily with flour on your hands so it won't stick."

YEAST, SUGAR, WATER, SALT, AND FLOUR

THE DOUGH SHOULD BE NICE AND SMOOTH

LET IT RISE A HALF HOUR UNDER A TOWEL

KNEAD, KNEAD AN FORM ROUND BUNS

28

first bread

I kneaded and kneaded for at least three minutes. The flour got all worked in, and the dough looked nice and smooth and moist (not sticky) on the outside.

"Don't knead it too much,"

said Stella. "The threads can be ruined if you do."

Stella greased a baking sheet, using a piece of paper towel with some butter on it. I rolled the dough into a sausage shape and then cut it into eight pieces. Stella and I formed them into round buns. Stella's were nice and smooth, and mine were wrinkled and ugly.

"Whew!" I said, when all the buns were in place on the baking sheet with a dish towel over them, ready for a second rising. "It's so hot I think I'll open the window . . ."

"Are you crazy!"

yelled Stella. "Drafts are the worst possible thing for yeast. They make the dough collapse."

After half an hour the dough had risen even more!

We had turned the oven on to 425°F a little earlier. Now we put the baking sheet in the middle of the oven. We left the buns in for 10 minutes before checking them.

"Not quite yet," said Stella, when she had lifted one up with a spatula. "It still feels 'heavy.' It should feel dry and light."

After 12 minutes the buns were done. They were "suntanned" on top, and they felt light when we picked them up.

We wrapped a dish towel around them and let them cool in a basket. Meanwhile, we cleaned up and made some tea.

Then we each cut a bun in half and buttered it. Who would have thought freshly baked bread could taste so good!!!

I wrote down the recipe in my recipe book.

8 Small White Buns

1 package active dry yeast ($^1/_4$ oz.)
$^1/_4$ tsp. sugar
1 cup warm water (110°-115° F)
$^1/_2$ tsp. salt
$2^1/_2$ cups flour

- Soak the yeast and sugar in a little warm water.
- Add the rest of the water and salt.
- Measure and stir in the flour, saving $^1/_4$ cup.
- Let it rise a half hour covered with a dish towel.
- Grease a baking sheet.
- Knead the dough with the rest of the flour (not too long).
- Form into 8 balls and put on the baking sheet.
- Let them rise under a dish towel for a half hour.
- Turn the oven on to 425°F.
- Bake for 10–15 minutes.

LET THEM RISE A HALF HOUR ON THE BAKING SHEET

TURN THE OVEN ON TO 425° F

BAKE FOR 10-15 MINUTES

EAT WITH BUTTER AND JAM. WHAT A FEAST!

More wheat breads

Shell
Husk
Kernel
Sprout

This is what a grain of cereal looks like inside. Ordinary flour is made from grinding only the kernel of a grain of wheat. The shell, husk, and sprout are all thrown away.

The next time we baked we used *whole-wheat flour*: flour that's ground using the *whole* wheat grain. That's why whole-wheat flour looks a little coarser and darker than regular flour. The bread turned out really well. "It's good for you, too," said Stella, "because it has more fiber, vitamins, and minerals than ordinary white bread." But whole-grain bread (baked from the *whole* grain) needs more time to rise.

Whole-Wheat Braid

1 package active dry yeast (¼ oz.)
¼ tsp. sugar
1 cup warm water (110°-115° F)
½ tsp. salt
1¼ cups whole-wheat flour
1¼ cups white flour

HERE'S WHAT WE DID:
• We mixed the dough exactly the way we did when we made the small white buns (see pages 28 and 29). When we mixed in the flour, we used the whole-wheat flour first and then the white flour (saving ¼ cup).
• We let the dough rise for 2 whole hours. (If you're in a hurry, you can get away with 1 hour.)
• We didn't make buns this time. Instead, we divided the dough into three parts, and then rolled them into long sausage shapes (an inch or so thick and about 15 inches long). Then we braided them together into one braid, and let it rise under a dish towel for half an hour.

We baked the braid at 400°F for 30 minutes or so (on a lower shelf).

When the bread cooled, we cut a slice and put butter on it. Super-good!

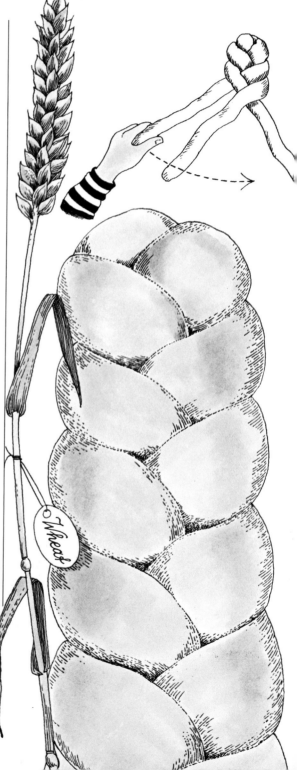

Wheat

Cinnamon Rolls (delicious)

We baked sweet rolls, too, from dough that has more sugar in it. You eat them without butter, but they're not a bit good for you, even though they taste WONDERFUL!
Makes 12

FOR THE DOUGH:

¼ cup butter (or margarine)
1 cup milk
1 package active dry yeast (¼ oz.)
¼ tsp. and ¼ cup sugar
1 tsp. ground cardamom
3 cups flour

FOR THE FILLING:

3 tbsp. butter (or margarine)
3 tbsp. sugar
1 tsp. ground cinnamon (comes from the bark of a tree that grows in Asia)

HERE'S WHAT WE DID:

• We took ¼ cup or half a stick of butter and heated it gently in a pan to melt it.

• As soon as the butter was all melted, we poured in the milk and heated it until it was warm. Then we poured it into a large mixing bowl and added the yeast, which had been soaked in a little warm water, and ¼ tsp. sugar. We mixed it all together with a wooden spoon.

• Next we added the ¼ cup sugar and cardamom.

• And then the flour. We had measured out 3 cups, and we mixed in all but ¼ cup.

When the dough was nice and smooth, we let it rise 40 minutes in the bowl, covered with a dish towel.

• Then, after kneading the dough a couple of minutes, I rolled it out with a rolling pin dusted with flour. (If you don't have a rolling pin, you can use a bottle.)

• Meanwhile, Stella mixed the filling together in a cup: butter, sugar, and cinnamon.

• I used a spatula to spread the filling evenly on the dough. Then I rolled it up.

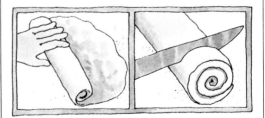

• I cut thick slices of the rolled-up dough and put them in cupcake papers. I got 12 one-inch-thick slices from the roll. I let the end pieces be a little thicker (they would have looked too skimpy otherwise).

• I put the buns on a baking sheet and covered them with the dish towel and let them rise for half an hour.

• When they were almost ready, we set the oven at 425°F. Then we put the baking sheet in the middle of the oven and baked them for about 10 minutes (they may be done even faster). They were golden brown and smelled heavenly!

31

A loaf of rye...

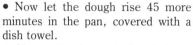

Now I'll tell you about my rye bread. It's baked with coarse whole-grain rye flour (which you can buy in health food stores). But you can't use *only* rye flour. The dough would be too sticky and hard to handle, and it wouldn't rise very well either. You have to add some white flour.

Most cookbooks say that you should use milk (instead of water) and butter. I tried making it that way, but I thought it was harder. Here's my own recipe instead:

1 package active dry yeast ($^1/_4$ oz.)
$^1/_4$ tsp. sugar
1 cup warm water (110°-115° F)
$^1/_2$ tsp. salt
$^3/_4$ cup coarse rye flour
$1^1/_4$ cups white flour (plus a little more for working the dough)

HERE'S WHAT YOU DO:

• Pour the packet of dry yeast into a bowl. Add the sugar and some of the warm water. Stir until the yeast is dissolved. Then add the rest of the water and the salt.
• Add the rye flour.
• Add the white flour, stirring with a wooden fork until you get a nice even dough.
• Cover the dough with a dish towel and let it rise. This kind of dough will take about 2 hours.
• Grease a loaf pan with butter, using a piece of paper towel.
• Turn the dough out onto a clean surface sprinkled with flour. Knead. It will be harder and stickier to work with than dough made from only white flour.
• Shape the dough into a loaf and put it into the greased pan.
• And now, here comes the fun part: cutting a braid pattern in the dough. With a scissors, cut small flaps in the loaf and then fold them back, first to the right, then to the left.

• Now let the dough rise 45 more minutes in the pan, covered with a dish towel.
• About 10 minutes before baking, set the oven at 400°F.
• Large loaves baked in pans take longer than small rolls. That's why a loaf of rye bread takes as long as 40-45 minutes. Bake on a lower oven rack, but not on the bottom one.

To check if the bread is done, I take it out of the oven (using pot holders) and turn the pan upside down, so the bread falls out. If it feels light and is dry on the bottom, then it's done. It's usually a little suntanned on the top, too.

...and oat scones

Arthur and I often bake scones when we come home from school hungry. They're really fast to make because they don't need to rise.

Instead of yeast, we use baking powder, which makes the dough rise in the oven. We bake the scones as soon as the dough is mixed.

This recipe is for a small batch (just right for Arthur and me), because bread made with baking powder doesn't stay fresh and should be eaten right away.

HERE'S WHAT YOU NEED:

½ cup oatmeal
⅔ cup white flour
1 tsp. baking powder
⅛ tsp. salt
2 tbsp. butter (or margarine)
½ cup milk

HERE'S WHAT YOU DO:

- Set the oven at 475°F.
- Mix the dry ingredients in a bowl: oatmeal, flour, baking powder, and salt.
- Cut thin slices of the butter (it should be cold and hard) and mix them with the dry ingredients in the bowl. Use your fingertips and work quickly, until everything looks like small crumbs.
- Pour in the cold milk and stir quickly. As soon as it has become a dough, put it on a greased baking sheet and shape it into a sticky round bun. Flatten it a little and make a cross on the top with a dull knife. That makes it easier to divide later.
- Put the baking sheet on a rack in the middle of the oven and bake 10-12 minutes. The bread will swell up to twice its size!

- When it is ready, and has cooled a little, we each take two pieces. We split each piece to make sandwiches that we first spread with butter. Then Arthur puts cheese on two of his and marmalade on the others. I usually have two with cheese and two with HONEY (because I like it so much). We drink tea (page 36) with our sandwiches and a glass of milk.

Bread seasonings

Anise, fennel, and *caraway seeds* are good bread seasonings, by themselves or used together (1 tsp. is plenty). *Saffron* is good in sweet breads. It makes them turn yellow. Saffron is expensive, because it's made from the stigmas of the saffron crocus, and it takes lots of them to make one little packet of saffron.

Surprise tart

Custard Sauce

HERE'S WHAT YOU NEED:

1 egg
2 tbsp. flour
¼ cup sugar
1¼ cups milk
½ tsp. vanilla
½ cup whipping cream

Now I'll tell you about Stella's birthday. I surprised her in the morning with an apple tart with custard sauce. And a little song. The tart, the sauce, and the song were all homemade (the night before).

APPLE TART:

½ cup whole-wheat flour
½ cup white flour
6 tbsp. butter
2 apples
1 tbsp. sugar
1 tsp. cinnamon

HERE'S WHAT I DID:

• I preheated the oven to 425°F.
• I put the two flours in a mixing bowl. I cut the butter into thin slices (it should be cold and hard) and added them to the flour.
• I quickly rubbed the butter into the flour (using my fingertips), until everything looked like small crumbs.
• I spread the crumbs out evenly in a little (6-inch) pie pan and pressed them down.
• I cut the apples into quarters and took out the cores. Then I cut the quarters into thin slices that I arranged in a circle on top of the dough.
• I mixed the sugar and cinnamon together and sprinkled them over the apples.
• I baked the tart for about 20 minutes in the oven.

for Stella

HERE'S WHAT I DID:

• I put the egg, flour, sugar, and milk in a pan and beat them until they were mixed. (If you use an aluminum pan, you have to beat them with a wooden spoon or fork. Metal beaters will make the sauce turn gray.)

• I warmed the sauce carefully until it started to thicken. I stirred it all the time so it wouldn't stick to the bottom. You can't let the sauce boil, or it will suddenly get lumpy.

• When the sauce had cooled, I stirred in the vanilla.

The next morning

I got up early and beat the whipping cream until it was thick. Then I stirred in the custard sauce and poured it all into a pitcher.

I PUT THE TART
AND THE
CUSTARD SAUCE
ON A TRAY
AND WENT UP
TO STELLA'S.
I SANG MY
HOMEMADE SONG
(SECRET).
GUESS IF SHE
WAS SURPRISED!

35

Yum, yum

BOY AM I TIRED!

LET'S GO TO MY HOUSE AND MAKE A SNACK

Snacks are really important. When we come home from school in the afternoon, we're both tired and hungry.

If we're *really* tired, we just take a glass of milk, a sandwich, and some fruit. But usually it's more fun to make something. We make different things every day.

Here you can see what we made today, yesterday, and the day before yesterday. You can use your own ideas for your snacks.

Choose whatever you like, but *always* try to include something with *protein* (milk, cheese, egg, meat), *fiber* (whole-grain bread, vegetables), and *vitamins* (fruit, vegetables). The rest of what you need will usually just sort of slip in by itself.

Yogurt with sliced banana, ham and cucumber sandwich, and a cup of tea

But not just any old tea. I make it like this, and it's much better than using tea bags:

- I heat up as many cups of water as I want in a pan or kettle.

- While it's heating, I put some tea leaves in a teapot, one teaspoonful for every cup of water.

- When the water starts to boil, I turn off the heat and pour the water over the leaves in the teapot. Then the tea should steep for 5 minutes, so all the flavor comes out. If it draws any longer, though, it can taste bitter.

- I pour the tea into my cup through a little strainer, so I won't get any leaves in it. Tea grows on bushes high up on warm mountain slopes in Asia. Most tea comes from India, Sri Lanka, China, Japan, the Soviet Union, and Africa.

After water, tea is the world's most common drink. That's both because it tastes good and because it's cheap.

The tea they put in tea bags is not the best quality.

Tea has been around for thousands of years. You'll find a story about tea on page 56.

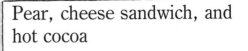

Crêpes (thin pancakes), vanilla cottage cheese, cranberry sauce, a glass of milk, and a carrot

FOR 10 (SMALL) CRÊPES YOU'LL NEED:

1 egg
¹/₂ cup flour
1 ¹/₃ cups milk
Pinch of salt
1 tbsp. butter

HERE'S WHAT YOU DO:

• Crack the egg into a bowl. Add the flour and beat until very smooth.
• Beat the milk into the batter, a little at a time. Add the salt.
• Take out a small frying pan (crêpes always fall apart when I make them in a big pan) and melt the butter over low heat. Pour it into the batter. When you have butter in the batter, you don't have to grease the pan with every new crêpe. The butter left in the pan from when you melted it is enough for the first crêpe. You should let the batter stand awhile and swell up a little before you make the crêpes.
• Heat up the pan. Mix the batter and pour some into the frying pan (or use a ladle to scoop out a small portion of the batter for each crêpe). Rock the pan a little so the batter will spread out evenly. When the crêpe is no longer shiny, it's time to turn it over with a spatula. Cook it just as long on the other side.
• We put cranberry sauce and cottage cheese on our crêpes. We flavored the cottage cheese with a few drops of vanilla and some confectioners' sugar (1 tsp. to ¹/₂ cup cottage cheese).

Pear, cheese sandwich, and hot cocoa

I'd better tell you how to make cocoa from scratch, because most people only know about the instant kind.
 Cacao pods grow on trees in Africa and South and Central America. Inside the pods are seeds which are roasted, peeled, and ground to make cocoa and chocolate.

HERE'S WHAT YOU NEED FOR 1 CUP:

1 large cup of milk
1 tsp. cocoa powder
2 tsp. sugar

HERE'S WHAT YOU DO:

• Pour the milk into a pot.
• Mix the cocoa powder and sugar in the cup. Pour in a *little* of the milk and stir until smooth.
• Warm the milk on the stove, keeping an eye on it. Take it off before it boils. Pour it into the cup and stir.
• Put some water in the pot right away, so it won't be hard to wash later.
 I usually dip my sandwich in my cocoa, which makes the cocoa run down my chin. (It's a good idea to use a paper napkin, because the stains are hard to get out.)

Archie's Special

Stella learned this recipe from her husband, Archie, and she taught it to us. Archie made everything in one pan when he was out at sea (fewer dishes to do).

Archie usually added an egg and some chopped onion to the ground beef when he made his "special." But Arthur doesn't like onions, and he thinks an egg makes the meat patties too soft, so we don't make it exactly the way Archie did. Different people have different tastes. (You can see how to chop an onion on page 41.)

THIS IS WHAT YOU'LL NEED FOR
TWO PEOPLE:

¹/₂ lb. ground beef
Salt and pepper
A small bunch of dill
Butter for frying
1 small can green peas (about 8 oz.)

HERE'S WHAT YOU DO:

• Season the meat with salt and pepper. Form it into 4 flat round meat patties (Stella usually makes a crisscross pattern on them with a spatula).
• Melt some butter in a big frying pan. When it's all melted and has stopped sputtering, add the patties. Fry them well on each side, letting them get brown all the way through.
• While the meat is frying, open the can of peas and pour them into the pan, water and all. There will be a lot of sputtering. Turn down the heat. Let everything simmer until it's all warm.
• Chop the dill and sprinkle it over the meat and peas. Serve your "special" right away, with boiled potatoes (see page 6).

A CAN OF PEAS
AND LOTS OF DILL
FOR ARCHIE'S
SPECIAL

Arthur and I take turns inviting each other for dinner. Sometimes Stella joins us. We plan the menu ahead of time, so we'll have everything we need. We've decided that no one is allowed to make the same thing twice in a row. Sometimes we work together on a meal.

Here are some of the dinners we've made:

Sailor's Boat

Here's something that Stella and Archie made up when they were out in a little boat and had only one pan to cook with.

I usually use *fresh* codfish fillet, because I like to go to the fish market. Besides, fresh fish tastes a *little* better than frozen fish. But Arthur wants me to mention that there can be bones in a fresh fish fillet. You usually won't find any bones in a frozen fish fillet.

HERE'S WHAT YOU NEED FOR ONE PERSON:

2 medium-size potatoes
1 cod fillet (fresh or frozen)
1 tomato
1-inch slice of leek
Pepper and a tiny bit of salt
Some small dabs of butter
Aluminum foil

HERE'S WHAT YOU DO:

• Wash the potatoes well and put them in a big pan. Fill the pan with water so it just covers the potatoes.
• Cut off about 12 inches of foil and grease it in the middle (where the fish will be). Use a little butter on a piece of paper towel. Be careful not to make a hole in the aluminum foil, or all the good sauce (that builds up inside the package) will run out into the water.
• Put the cod fillet on the foil and sprinkle it with salt and pepper. Wash and slice the tomato and put it over the fish. Rinse the leek and cut it into thin rings. Put those on top.
• *Carefully* fold the foil, wrapping it around the fish to make a tight little boat. Put the boat on top of the potatoes and turn on the heat.
• When the water starts boiling, turn down the heat and put a lid on the pan. Don't let it boil over.
• When the potatoes are done (15 to 20 minutes – test them), the fish will also be done (even if it was frozen).
• Lift out the boat *carefully* and open it a little. Check if the fish is nice and white. (Raw fish is more transparent.)
• Open the foil all the way *on your plate.* That way you won't lose any of the good juices from the fish and vegetables.

PUT THE FISH ON GREASED ALUMINUM FOIL

FOLD THE EDGES OVER A FEW TIMES

TWIST THE ENDS...

...LIKE THIS

PUT THE "BOAT" ON TOP OF THE POTATOES

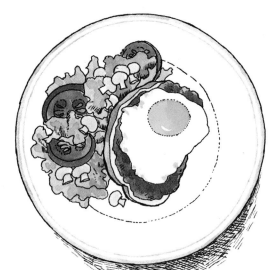

Nelson's Temptation

Stella makes a potato casserole with anchovies that's called Janson's Temptation. But I use smoked ham instead of anchovies and call it Nelson's Temptation.

NELSON'S TEMPTATION FOR TWO:
Butter to grease the baking dish
6 medium-size potatoes
2-inch slice of leek
4 slices of smoked ham
½ cup whipping cream
½ cup milk

HERE'S WHAT YOU DO:
● Heat the oven to 425°F.
● Grease an *ovenproof* baking dish with some butter on a paper towel.
● Peel the potatoes. Cut 2 potatoes up into small sticks (cutting first lengthwise and then across). Put the sticks in the bottom of the baking dish.
● Rinse the leek and cut it into thin rings. Put half the rings on top of the potato sticks.
● Cut 2 ham slices into long strips and put them in the dish.
● Make another layer with 2 potatoes, leek slices, and ham strips. Finish off with a top layer of 2 potatoes.
● Pour the cream and milk over the whole thing. (You can forget about the cream and use only milk. It won't be as good, but it won't be as fattening either.)
● Put the baking dish in the oven. It took 35 minutes the last time I made my temptation, but you can check on it after half an hour. The potatoes should be soft when you prick them, and they should have a golden-brown color. Then Nelson's Temptation is ready. Eat a salad with it.

NELSON
TEMPTS
ME MORE
THAN
JANSON

Parisian Hamburger

An easy-to-make meal. I usually have room for only one, but some people can eat two.

FOR TWO PARISIAN HAMBURGERS YOU'LL NEED:
½ small onion
¼ lb. ground meat
2 slices white bread
Butter for frying
2 eggs
Salt and pepper

HERE'S WHAT YOU DO:
● Chop the onion as small as you can (read how on page 41). Mix the chopped onion with the ground meat.
● Toast the bread.
● Spread the ground meat on the toast; press it down firmly, letting it hang over the edges a little. (It will shrink when it's fried.)
● Warm a big frying pan and put in some butter. When the butter has melted and stopped sputtering, put in the hamburgers (*meat side down*) and fry for a few minutes.
● Crack 2 eggs and fry them in the pan at the same time (if you have room; otherwise, use another pan for the eggs). You may have to add more butter first so the eggs won't stick to the pan.
● Turn the hamburgers over with a spatula. Add some salt and pepper and put them on a plate. Put an egg on top of each one. Now they are Parisian Hamburgers. You can have pickled beets and capers with them if you want.

WHEN YOU CHOP ONIONS, YOU GET TO HAVE A GOOD CRY

Beet-Red Soup

This Russian soup is really called *borscht* and gets its color from red beets. There are some special spices in it, too. Arthur is not so sure about this soup, but I like it.

CUT THE ONION IN HALF FIRST. NEXT CUT IT LENGTHWISE, AND THEN CROSSWISE

BEET BORSCHT FOR TWO:

3 medium-size beets
1 medium-size onion
2 tbsp. butter
½ cup chopped cabbage
2½ cups water
1 bouillon cube
1 bay leaf
2 cloves
1 tsp. vinegar
A little salt, maybe
Parsley
½ cup sour cream

HERE'S WHAT YOU DO:

• Peel 2 beets and grate them with a cheese grater (using the side with the biggest holes). Be careful of your fingers.

• Chop the onion into small pieces.
• Melt the butter in a big pot. When it has stopped sputtering, add the grated beets, onion, and cabbage. Stir to keep from burning. Let it cook for a few minutes.
• Add water, the bouillon cube, bay leaf, and cloves. Let it all come to a boil and then turn down the heat. Let it *simmer* for half an hour with a lid on the pot.
• Peel and grate the third beet and add it when the soup is ready. Then put in the vinegar, salt, and finely chopped parsley. Remove the bay leaf.
• Add a dab of sour cream just before serving. I usually make some open-face cheese sandwiches and heat them in the oven when the soup is almost done. They're nice to eat with the soup.

A section on sauce

Sauce Green

(*Sauce verte* in French, pronounced "sohss vairt"). You eat this green sauce cold, on fish, for example.

THIS IS WHAT YOU'LL NEED:
10-oz. package of frozen spinach (chopped, but not creamed)
1 cup sour cream
2 tbsp. mayonnaise
2 tbsp. or more cress, dill, or parsley (whichever you want)
1/2 tsp. dried tarragon and a little salt and pepper

- Thaw the frozen spinach in a strainer.
- Mix the sour cream and mayonnaise in a bowl.
- Squeeze out as much water as you can from the thawed spinach. Press it with a big spoon.
- Add the spinach to the sour cream and mayonnaise.
- Add chopped cress, dill, or parsley if you like.
- Season the sauce and let it sit in the refrigerator awhile before you serve it.

WARM FISH SANDWICH WITH GREEN SAUCE!

Sauce White

(*Sauce Béchamel* in French, pronounced "sohss bay-shah-*mell*"). Some people say that it's hard to make white sauce. But that's not true. It's easy if you make it like this:

HERE'S WHAT YOU'LL NEED:
1 tbsp. butter (or margarine)
1 tbsp. flour
2/3 cup milk
Salt and pepper

HERE'S WHAT YOU DO:
- Carefully melt the butter in a small pot. Turn down the heat. Add the flour. Mix it in with a whisk or a wooden spoon. Stir it all the time so it doesn't burn or get lumpy. Take the pot off the heat if it gets too warm.
- Pour in *all* the milk. Heat the sauce, stirring all the time, until it becomes thick and smooth.
- Now you can season it. Use salt and pepper, or slice in some cheese (try Swiss or another firm cheese) and let it melt in the sauce.
- Try pouring the cheese sauce over slightly cooked cauliflower and putting it in the oven (475°F) for 10 minutes. Arthur likes to eat it with fried hot dogs.

YOU CAN HAVE HOT DOGS (FANCIER WITH THE ENDS SNIPPED) WITH YOUR CAULIFLOWER

Rice – the grain of life

No plant feeds as many people as rice, Stella says. In many places in the world, people would starve to death if it wasn't for rice. That's why I call it the *Grain of Life*.

Rice is grown in warm countries, mostly in Asia, but also in the United States and Italy. The rice is planted, plant by plant, in shallow paddies, with just the tops sticking up above the water. As the rice grows, more water is added, but at harvest time the water is drained off the paddies.

Rice has been grown for thousands of years. A hundred years ago, a new disease was discovered called *beriberi*. It was killing thousands, and people believed it was contagious (catching). But that wasn't true. People were getting sick because they had started to peel (polish) rice. They didn't understand that when rice became nice and white, it also lost all its vitamin B, which was stored in the brown coating! That's why people were getting beriberi. Rice was practically their only source of vitamins.

Today we can buy unpolished rice. It's called brown rice. It cooks a little slower than polished rice and it doesn't fall apart as easily.

If you see rice that is marked *parboiled* or *converted,* this is what it means: the rice has first been treated with steam under high pressure to force some of the vitamins and minerals into the kernel. Converted rice doesn't get sticky.

When you are cooking rice to eat as part of a meal, you should use *long-grained rice*. It will be dry and fluffy when it's cooked. For rice pudding you can use a short, round rice that will be stickier when cooked.

Cooking rice

FOR ONE PORTION:

$^1/_4$ *cup rice*
Pinch of salt
$^1/_2$ *cup water*

HERE'S WHAT YOU DO:

• Heat the salt and water in a pot until the water boils. Add the rice.
• Turn down the heat as low as you can. The rice should now cook very slowly for 20 minutes (with a lid on). DON'T TAKE OFF THE LID! DON'T STIR THE RICE! DON'T EVEN PEEK! One of the things that makes the rice cook is the steam in the pot. If you take the cover off, you let out the steam.
• A trick for keeping the heat really low is to put three pennies on the burner (electric stove only!).
• After 20 minutes the rice should be dry and fluffy. The grains have swelled up much bigger than the tiny little portion you put in the pot to begin with.
• I eat fish, meat, or vegetables with rice. Sometimes I make a meat sauce (see page 53) and put it on cooked rice instead of on spaghetti.

Is there enough

"**M**any people in this world eat *nothing but* a bowl of rice for dinner," said Stella, "without even the tiniest piece of meat in it."

"Isn't there enough meat for everybody?" asked Arthur. "How many people are there in the world?"

"Can you live on *nothing but* rice?" I asked.

Stella couldn't answer all those questions, so we took off for the library again. We didn't find any children's books on the world's food production, but Stella found some in the adult section that we checked out.

5 billion people

That's how many we are on the earth. If you want to write it out in numbers, you need nine zeros:

5,000,000,000

About one billion people are thought to be undernourished. That means that every *fifth* person on earth doesn't get enough to eat. *Three-quarters* of them are children. Many are so undernourished that they get sick and die. In the worst cases, there is no food at all for anyone.

There would be enough food if everyone could afford it,

but everyone can't. In our country we can grow and buy more food than we need. But many countries are so poor that they don't have enough food for all their people.

In some countries, such as India, there is enough food for everyone. Yet only *some* people there can afford to eat until they are full, while most people still get too little to eat. It is like that in some "wealthy" countries like the United States, as well.

So it's the unfair division of money *between* countries and *within* countries that makes one out of five people not get enough to eat. If all people were able to buy or grow their own food, then no one would have to starve.

Why is it so unfair?

Many countries could raise enough food to feed everyone in their own country. But instead they raise other things that can't be eaten, like cotton, tobacco, and coffee.

Rich landowners and big companies decide what to plant in the fields. They earn more money selling these things to other countries than by raising food for their own people.

"And people go along with that!" said Arthur.

"They're not allowed to help decide," said Stella. "The ones with the most money decide the most. Even though there are more poor people."

"How *crazy*!" I said.

"Yes, if you think about it," said Stella, "it really is crazy."

food for everyone in the world?

Expensive protein – and cheap protein

"If we divided up all the food fairly, would everybody get to eat hot dogs every day?" asked Arthur.

"Hardly," said Stella. "Meat protein is expensive. Think about it: first we have to use the fields to raise food for animals: beef cattle, for example. When the cows have eaten and gotten big, we slaughter them, and it's only *then* that we can eat them and get our protein. But if we had raised food for ourselves in the same fields, we would have gotten *five times* as much protein. And we wouldn't have had to use the cows to get it."

"Oh," I said. "Well, which plants have protein, then?"

"Legumes and grains, for example," said Stella.

"LEGUMES! Is that something to eat?" said Arthur.

"GRAIN! That sounds like chicken food," I said.

"Peas and beans and lentils are all legumes," said Stella. "And wheat, rye, oats, and barley are all grains. Rice is also a grain."

"Shouldn't there be *any* cows at all?" I asked. That would be a little sad, I thought.

"Oh yes, but not as many as now. We could raise them in order to get milk and cheese. Milk protein is high quality and not as expensive as meat protein, since we get so much from each cow. Sheep, goats, chickens, and a pig or two would be nice to have, too."

How will it be in the future?

If you measure out about half a cup of dried beans and two cups of brown rice, and then cook them and eat them in one day, you've gotten as much protein as you would have from a big piece of meat (weighing about half a pound). That's cheap! And it's more protein than an adult man needs for one day. But *only* beans or *only* rice is not enough. You have to eat some of *both*, at *every* meal, to make the different kinds of protein work together in the right way. (You have to eat a lot of other things to stay healthy, too. We already talked about that on page 10.)

"In the future, will we have to become vegetarians in order for there to be enough food?" asked Arthur.

"Well, I'm not sure about that," said Stella. "Today there is already more than enough food for all the people on earth. But we take better care of Mother Earth if we don't eat meat. That way, we don't have to grow as much food in order for there to be enough food for everyone."

"But do beans and rice *taste* good?" asked Arthur.

"There are lots of other plants you could choose," said Stella. "If we were used to eating plant protein from the beginning, we probably wouldn't even think that meat was all that good."

"Do you mean that in fifty years we won't even be able to have a little spaghetti with meat sauce on our birthday?" I asked.

"Well, maybe so," said Stella. "It takes time to get people to change their eating habits. But who knows, maybe we'll have learned to cook with new foods by then, and we'll think they're just as good as your old meat sauce . . .

"But most important of all is that we all do what we can to end world hunger."

Stella, Arthur,

Dough for Bread Twists

We planned on baking the bread at our picnic site, but we mixed the dough before we left and packed it in a plastic bag to take with us.

FOR 6 BREAD TWISTS YOU'LL NEED:

1 1/2 cups flour
1/2 tsp. salt
2 tsp. baking powder
1/4 cup (2 oz.) butter
1/2 cup milk

HERE'S WHAT YOU DO:

• Mix the flour, salt, and baking powder in a bowl.

• Slice the butter (it should be hard and cold) into the mixing bowl. Using your fingertips, rub the butter into the flour until you get a crumbly mixture (like the tart dough on page 34).

• Add the milk, mixing as little as possible.

• Put the dough into a plastic bag and close it with a clothespin or a rubber band.

Now I'll tell you about our picnic in the woods last fall. We planned the menu the day before. We decided to have fried chicken legs, bread twists, some raw vegetables, and a few other goodies.

Stella thawed out the frozen chicken legs the night before and fried two of them for each of us. She seasoned them with *rosemary*, pepper, and salt, and then fried them over low heat, a little longer than it said on the package (we *didn't* want chicken legs that were pink on the inside).

The next morning Stella wrapped some aluminum foil around the bone ends, so we could use them like handles when we ate the chicken legs.

We carried the food in two baskets and Arthur's plastic bucket. We also took a real tablecloth and some newspapers to sit on. And Stella packed a "mystery bag."

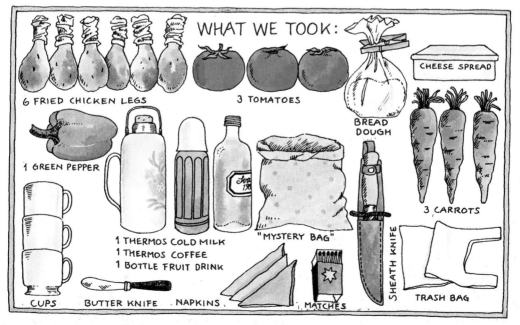

WHAT WE TOOK:

6 FRIED CHICKEN LEGS

3 TOMATOES

CHEESE SPREAD

BREAD DOUGH

3 CARROTS

1 GREEN PEPPER

1 THERMOS COLD MILK
1 THERMOS COFFEE
1 BOTTLE FRUIT DRINK

"MYSTERY BAG"

SHEATH KNIFE

TRASH BAG

CUPS   BUTTER KNIFE   NAPKINS   MATCHES

A SHEATH KNIFE WITH A METAL BAR ACROSS THE BLADE IS BEST
(THEN YOU DON'T CUT YOURSELF AS EASILY IF THE KNIFE SLIPS)

and I go on a picnic

Our picnic

We took the bus to a picnic spot Stella knew about. It was in the woods and you were allowed to make a fire by the creek.

Arthur and I made a fire, and while it was burning down to coals, we looked for some sticks (not too dry) to roast the bread on. We divided the dough into six pieces and rolled each one into a long snake between our hands. Then we twisted the snakes around the sticks and roasted them over the coals.

Wow, the dough really puffed up! We could roast only one at a time because they had to be turned all the time to keep from burning. They should get only *slightly* brown.

Our bread twists turned out really well. We put some cheese spread on them. The chicken legs were good, too. And the raw vegetables. We ate until we were stuffed.

After we'd eaten, Stella took out her "mystery bag." It was full of fat juicy plums. We stretched out on the ground, eating our plums and looking up at the clouds. Stella drank some coffee.

Then it was time to put out the fire. Stella explained that the roots underground *can* start to burn without our seeing it. To be on the safe side, we filled our bottle with some water from the creek and poured it over the fire.

Then we were ready to pack up and wait for the bus back to town.

We make

Stella and Arthur and I bought some fresh cranberries to make cranberry relish. After we'd thrown out the ones that were bad, we rinsed the berries and put them in a big brown stoneware jar that Stella had.

We added some sugar. Stella said we should use about $\frac{1}{2}$ cup sugar for each pint (2 cups) of cranberries.

We took turns chopping and stirring the berries. You have to stir until all the sugar is dissolved. It's good idea to stir even longer than that.

The relish that we made is uncooked. It won't keep as long as cooked jam, but you can freeze it. (If it lasts that long. But it probably won't, because it's so super-good.)

We stirred and stirred, and while we were stirring we played a game:

Arthur said Spaghetti, and then I was supposed to come up with a food word that began with the last letter in spaghetti.

"I-i-i-ice cream," I said.

"M-m-m-melon," said Stella.

"N-n-n-newsoup," said Arthur.

"There's no food called newsoup," I said.

"Oh yes, there is," said Arthur.

The next day we went up to Stella's with some empty jars. We washed them well, and then we filled them with relish.

If you use *clean* jars with *clean* lids that close tightly, and if you store them in a dark, cool

cranberry relish

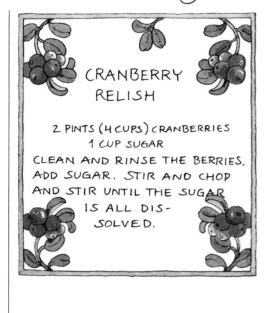

CRANBERRY RELISH

2 PINTS (4 CUPS) CRANBERRIES
1 CUP SUGAR
CLEAN AND RINSE THE BERRIES,
ADD SUGAR. STIR AND CHOP
AND STIR UNTIL THE SUGAR
IS ALL DIS-
SOLVED.

place, your cranberry relish can keep for a few months.

We made labels with the date for our relish jars. Stella showed us how to make "bonnets" for the jars. She cut out small squares of cloth and fastened them on top of the jar lids with rubber bands. That was just to make them look nice.

Using the relish

Cranberry cone – Whipped cream and cranberry relish in a sugar cone
Cranberry sandwich – Something Stella ate when she was a kid
Cranberry relish with milk – A good dessert
Cranberry relish on pancakes or waffles
Cranberry relish with meatballs or roast turkey or chicken

Fruit fun and

I like summer and fall because there are so many kinds of fruits in season then. I usually just eat them raw, but sometimes I bake or cook something with them. It's a good thing they're so good for you, because I eat a *lot*. Fruits are packed with vitamins and minerals, and both the flesh and the peels have lots of fiber.

Silver Bundle

- Turn the oven on to 435°F.
- Remove the core from an apple. Use a potato peeler, so there will be a hole going all the way through the apple.
- Make a filling from 1 tsp. sugar, 1 tsp. butter, and a little less than 1 tsp. cinnamon. Fill the apple hole with this mixture.
- Put the apple in the center of a piece of aluminum foil and wrap it up into a little bundle. Twist it closed on top.
- Put it in the oven (on a baking sheet) for about 15 minutes or longer. Yum! Sometimes I make custard sauce to go with the apple (see page 34).

Berry-Good Sandwich Spread

If you have some berries left over from dessert, try putting them in a pot with some sugar or honey. Let the mixture come to a boil. Then stir and cool. Pour it into a cup or glass jar and you'll have the best sandwich spread in the world.

Pear Porcupine

This recipe makes 4 porcupines (for 4 people).
- Set the oven at 435°F.
- Peel 2 pears and cut them in half lengthwise. Remove the core with a teaspoon.
- Cover the outside of the pear halves with almond paste (you'll need about a quarter pound).
- Stick slivered almonds in the pear halves so that they look like the needles on a porcupine. Add 2 raisins for eyes (on the narrower end).
- Bake in the oven (in an ovenproof dish) for 10–15 minutes.

This makes a fancy party dessert. It's even better with a little scoop of ice cream.

Archie's Oranges

Stella's husband, Archie, taught her to make this dessert. He learned how when he was in Morocco.

HERE'S WHAT YOU DO:
- Peel 2 oranges and cut them in slices. Arrange the slices nicely on a big platter. Sprinkle some cinnamon and a little sugar over them, and they're ready to eat! Makes enough for 2 to 4 people.

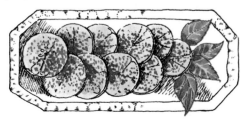

iceberg berries

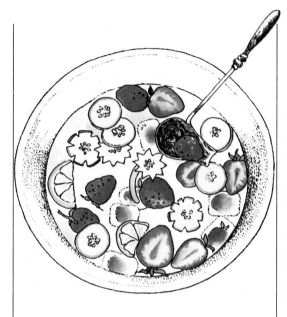

Summer Punch

Here's a good party punch for hot weather. You can use any kind of soda, but I usually make it with plain seltzer water and concentrated lemonade.

● Fill a punch bowl (or other large bowl) about half full with seltzer. Add the lemonade.

● Decorate with *strawberry halves, lemon slices, and cucumbers (cut in different shapes)* floating around on top of the seltzer.

● Add *ice cubes*.

● You'll need a big dipper to serve it, but even so, it can be pretty messy. Good thing I put my punch bowl (which was really our biggest salad bowl) on a tray.

Frozen Grapes

If you put some grapes in the freezer, you'll get small frozen grape balls you can use in fruit drinks (instead of ice cubes)!

Frozen Strawberry

I put a strawberry in a little plastic cup of water and stuck it in the freezer. The next day I had a strawberry ice cube to put in a big glass of fruit juice or some other drink.

Flower in a Glass

● Choose a tall, narrow glass. Cut a slice of lemon or orange and check to see if it will work as a stopper about halfway down in the glass.

● Put a pretty flower in the bottom of the glass. Carefully push the fruit slice down into the glass until it fits tightly against the sides, over the flower. Now you can pour in some fruit juice. It looks even nicer with a straw and a lemon slice hanging over the rim of the glass.

Stella learned how to do this from a Spanish cook named Ramón.

This is a good drink to make for someone you like a lot.

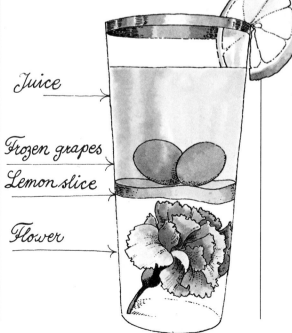

Juice

Frozen grapes

Lemon slice

Flower

First I decided what people I wanted to invite – Stella and Arthur, of course, and Linnea (you remember, my neighbor with the sprouts) and Mr. Bloom. Mr. Bloom is a friend of Linnea's. He's a gardener, and he's retired like Stella. We would be five people, counting me.

Next I decided on a menu (you'll see later) and made up a shopping list of what I needed to buy.

I also planned how I'd set the table. I remembered a table setting I had seen in a photograph. It was very fancy, with lots of glasses and knives and forks for everybody. The napkins were folded in a very elegant way. And there was an enormous silver fruit server – with a pineapple high up on top!

Well, I don't think I'll worry about making it all that fancy.

I didn't have a tablecloth, so I put everyone's plate on a paper doily instead. Then I set the table with the knives to the right, the forks to the left, and the dessert spoons above the plates, just as Stella taught me. You don't *have to* set the table that way, but it's not a bad idea (because then your guests can see that there will be dessert and leave room for it). I put the napkins in the glasses, sticking out at the top.

Then I made place cards for everybody, just for fun.

Now I'll tell you about the food.

party

First course: Vegetable dip

HERE'S WHAT I USED:

½ small cauliflower
2 carrots
3 pieces of celery
Dip: 1½ cups sour cream + seasonings

HERE'S WHAT I DID:

I rinsed the vegetables and divided the cauliflower into small "flowerets." I peeled the carrots with a potato peeler and cut them into sticks. I rinsed the celery and cut it into sticks, too. You can also use other vegetables cut up nicely: broccoli, cucumber, mushrooms, green and red peppers, for example.

I divided the sour cream into three different cups for the dips.

DIP NUMBER 1: I mixed in 1 tsp. chili sauce until it turned pink.

DIP NUMBER 2: I added a lot of chopped watercress to make a green polka-dot dip.

DIP NUMBER 3: I stirred in ½ tsp. dried herbs (try different combinations of oregano, basil, and tarragon, for example).

The idea, of course, is to dip the vegetables into the different dips.

Main course: Spaghetti and meat sauce

MEAT SAUCE

1 large onion
1 carrot
2 tbsp. butter (or olive oil) for frying
½ lb. ground beef
16-oz. can crushed tomatoes
½ tsp. oregano
½ tsp. salt and some pepper

10 oz. spaghetti (whole wheat is best), salt, and water

HERE'S WHAT I DID:

• I chopped the onion (see page 41) and grated the carrot (on the side of the grater with the largest holes). I melted half the butter in a big frying pan. When it stopped sputtering, I added the chopped onion and grated carrot. Then I cooked them over low heat, stirring all the time so they wouldn't burn, until the onion got sort of transparent. After that, I moved them over to a plate.

• I put the rest of the butter in the frying pan. When it had melted and stopped sputtering, I added the ground beef, breaking it up into small pieces with a fork. I kept the heat low this time, too, so the juice wouldn't all run out of the meat. When the meat was brown all the way through, I put the onion and carrot back into the frying pan.

• Now I opened the can of tomatoes and poured it all into the pan. That really made it sputter! Next I seasoned everything with oregano, salt, and pepper.

• Then I cooked the spaghetti in a big pot of salted, boiling water. The package tells you how long to cook the spaghetti.

• When the spaghetti is cooked, you drain off the water in a colander (see the picture on this page). Stella says *not* to rinse it in cold water; they don't do that in Italy, she says, and that's where spaghetti comes from. Put the spaghetti in a bowl (or back in the pot) and add a little olive oil or butter. You can also add some crushed dry oregano if you like.

I did everything *except* cook the spaghetti before the guests came.

FROM
MR. BLOOM
AND
ME

THERE'S
NOTHING WITH
CAPERS IN IT,
RIGHT?!

When everyone was sitting down at the table, I said, "Welcome!" And we drank a toast. We had lemon water (water with a squeeze of lemon and some ice cubes in it).

"Now I just have to go do a few things," I said, and went out to the kitchen and warmed up the meat sauce and got the spaghetti ready to serve.

"Delicious!" said Mr. Bloom.
"Wonderful sauce!" said Stella.
"May I have seconds?" asked Linnea.
"What's for dessert?" said Arthur.

Dessert:
Filled Pineapple

Earlier in the day I had cut a big pineapple in half and taken out the flesh. I cut it up in pieces and put it back into the pineapple halves, along with a sliced banana and some strawberry halves. It made a great fruit salad. You don't need any sugar because the pineapple itself is so sweet.

Well, that was my dinner party. Oh, I almost forgot – Stella and Mr. Bloom drank coffee after dinner, and then Stella played the accordion!

Oh, there's the doorbell! Imagine, everybody showed up at the same time!

And they all brought something: Linnea and Mr. Bloom gave me an amaryllis bulb that had just started growing. Stella had a bag of big juicy plums with her, and Arthur brought along his good humor.

First I brought in the tray with the dips and vegetables so everybody could try those.

And while they were doing that, I cooked the spaghetti.

Sometimes I have such a sweet tooth that I can't think of anything but sweets. But eating candy doesn't usually help; it just makes me hungry for more.

I read in a magazine why that happens: The sugar in candy goes right through your stomach and out into your intestines (see page 20). From your intestines it goes into your blood.

Since your body can't use all the sugar it's getting, your blood gets the extra, and that causes your blood-sugar level to go up.

And that sends a signal to a gland called the pancreas (right behind the stomach), which reacts by immediately producing something called *insulin.*

The insulin starts working to get rid of the extra blood sugar, but it works more than it should and goes too far. Oh oh! Now the blood-sugar level is *too low*!

That makes your body start craving sugar all over again, and you want to eat more candy. If you do that, your pancreas will make more insulin, you'll crave more sugar, and on and on it'll go.

Your blood-sugar level can be raised by food, too. That's why it's so common to crave something sweet after you've just eaten a meal.

A good way to fool your sweet tooth is to wait awhile. Most of the time the craving will just go away.

Too bad sweets aren't good for you

Everybody knows that you can get cavities from eating sweets. And most people have heard that the bacteria that make holes in your teeth need sugar in order to work. So here are some tips:

• It's better to eat lots of candy fast, and not very often, than to snack on small amounts all day long.

• Chocolate is better than chewy caramels or hard candies that you suck on a long time.

• Remember that soft drinks are also sweets.

• Sugarless gum is better than gum with sugar, since gum stays in your mouth such a long time.

• Brush your teeth well (and *immediately*) after eating sweets, so the sugar will not stay on your teeth.

• Spend your candy money on an exotic fruit instead of on sweets. Buy a kiwi fruit, cut it in half, and eat it with a spoon. Or buy a tangelo, an ugly but delicious cross between a grapefruit and a tangerine.

Elliot's Cocoa Crunch

After all that talk about sweets, here's a recipe for a gooey sweet snack. Sorry, but it's not one bit good for you (just like all sweets), so don't make it too often. And remember to brush your teeth right after you eat it. As you know, fat and sugar are not good for you, and corn flakes stick to your teeth.

HERE'S WHAT YOU'LL NEED:
2 tbsp. butter
2 tbsp. cocoa
2 tbsp. honey
$\frac{1}{2}$ cup corn flakes
10 cupcake papers

HERE'S WHAT YOU DO:
• Warm the butter, cocoa, and honey in a small pot, stirring until the butter is melted and everything is mixed together.

• Let it cool, and then add the corn flakes and stir until they are coated with the cocoa mixture.

• Spoon it into the cupcake papers. It usually takes about 10 papers, if you don't put too much in each one.

• Now the candies have to cool in the refrigerator. That takes at least half an hour. If you're lucky, your craving for sweets will be gone by then . . .

Odds and ends

Butter was best

"In the old days," said Stella, "butter was so expensive people couldn't afford to eat it every day. So they saved it for special occasions. It was especially important to have butter at Christmas time. Sometimes people made fancy shapes out of butter and used them for centerpieces on the table.

On Christmas Eve here in Sweden they went out to the barn and treated all the cows to bread and butter. That was to thank them for the milk they had so kindly given that year. And then the cows promised to keep on giving milk so that the butter would be just as good the coming year.

Pig tales

The meat we get from pigs is called pork. Ham, bacon, pork chops, and pork roast are all pig meat. Most pigs are raised in "factories," which are usually crowded and unpleasant for the poor pigs. They can suffer from such stress that they bite off each other's tail. And pigs that do still have tails usually don't have any curl in them. Pigs that have more space and lots of hay to play and sleep in, on the other hand, are content and have curly tails.

Who discovered tea?

Some 2,500 years ago, an Indian monk was traveling from India to China. One day he decided never to sleep again but to stay awake day and night and meditate instead.

But one night he was so tired that he fell asleep anyway. When he woke up, he was so disappointed in himself that he cut off his eyelids.

The next day he returned to the same place to meditate and found that his eyelids had rooted in the ground and become two bushes. The monk discovered that by making a drink from the leaves of these bushes, he could hold back sleep. (What a story!)

In the beginning, tea grew wild and got as big as trees. They say that tea was harvested in China by sending trained monkeys up into the trees to pick off the leaves and toss them down.

Nowadays tea leaves are picked by machines or by people. The trees are trimmed back to bush size, about 28 inches high.

In Japan, making and drinking tea is considered an art and there are special schools for learning how to do it. It can take up to three years to learn!

BODHIDHARMA THE PATRON OF THE TEA PLANT

Storing food

• *Vegetables and fruit* should be kept in a cool place, like the crisper drawer of your refrigerator. I rinse dill, parsley, and lettuce and put them in plastic bags before placing them in the refrigerator. I remove any wilted or spoiled leaves right away, so the rest will stay fresh. I usually keep tomatoes in a bowl in the kitchen, partly because they taste better then, and partly because they give off a gas that makes other vegetables spoil faster.

• *Potatoes and carrots* should be kept in a dark and cool place, but not in the refrigerator.

• Put *bread* in a plastic bag in a clean bread box. Crackers should be kept in a dry place.

• *Milk, cheese, other dairy products and eggs* should be kept in the refrigerator, of course.

• Keep *meat and fish* in the refrigerator, but not too long, or they can go bad and make you sick.

• *Flour and cereals* should be kept cool and dry.

• *Spices* need to be kept in a cool, dark, and dry place, so they won't lose their flavor. Don't save spices too long, because they won't have much taste then.

• Keep *butter and margarine* in the refrigerator in closed packages or in airtight containers, so they won't start tasting like other foods in the refrigerator.

Mold

Food that is kept too long can get moldy. You've probably seen that grayish-green fuzz that grows on bread, cheese, fruit, or vegetables. That's mold. Mold is a fungus and it is *not* good for you. When food gets moldy, throw it away. Don't just scrape away the part you can see, because the mold is already growing in the *whole* piece of cheese or loaf of bread, even if you don't see it.

about this and that

What is margarine?

Butter comes from the animal kingdom, but margarine is made mostly from plant and vegetable oils. Often it is made by pressing the seeds of different plants. Sunflowers, cottonseed, soy beans, and rapeseed are all plants rich in oil. You can also press oil from coconuts and palms.

After oil has been pressed out of the seeds, the rest can be used for animal food.

Sometimes animal fat, such as skim milk or fish oil, is added to margarine.

The oils are thickened when they are made into margarine, otherwise you wouldn't be able to spread them on your bread to make a sandwich.

Some tips about eggs

• To tell the difference between a raw and a cooked egg: Put the egg on a table and spin it. A cooked egg will spin quickly, while a raw egg will hardly spin at all.

• Fresh eggs taste best. The yolk of a fresh egg should be round and lie in the center of the white. An older egg has a flatter yolk and a thinner white.

Book tips

Here are some books we borrowed from the library. (You can also look in your local bookstore – especially if your birthday is coming up!)

• *Joy of Cooking,* by Irma S. Rombauer and Marion Rombauer Becker (New York: Macmillan Publishing Company, 1975).
This 900-page book will give you a recipe for almost anything. It also tells you everything from what cholesterol is to how to set your table properly.

• *The Moosewood Cookbook,* by Mollie Katzen (Berkeley: Ten Speed Press, 1977).
An adult cookbook that is fun and easy to follow. The mostly vegetarian (no meat!) recipes are from all over the world.

• *My First Cookbook: A Life-size Guide to Making Fun Things to Eat,* by Angela Wilkes (New York: Alfred A. Knopf, 1989).
An easy-to-follow cookbook for beginners who want more recipes once they've tried all of mine!

• *Diet for a Small Planet,* by Francis M. Lappe (New York: Ballantine Books, 1985).
An adult book about how we could provide enough protein for everyone on earth. It also has lots of healthy recipes.

• *The Color Atlas of Human Anatomy* (New York: Harmony Books, 1979).
This book has over 450 color photographs and drawings of all parts of the human body. It also tells you about how people investigate different parts of the body and what tools they use, from X rays to the electron microscope.

• *Why Do Our Bodies Stop Growing?: Questions about Human Anatomy Answered by the Natural History Museum,* by Dr. Philip Whitfield and Dr. Ruth Whitfield (New York: Viking Penguin, 1988).
Find out more about how we digest food or how we sneeze, run, or hear.

• *Animal Factories,* by Jim Mason and Peter Singer (New York: Crown Publishers, 1990).
An adult book about the terrible things that happen to animals on "factory farms." I could hardly bear to look at the pictures.

Last but not least

I *hate* getting up in the morning. But just when I've decided to crawl back under the covers again, I remember something: *I'm invited to breakfast!*

Well, it's only myself who's invited me, but so what . . .

I usually plan my breakfast the night before. And then I set the table with all the things I'll need.

Stella was the one who taught me that trick. She says that a good breakfast is a good way to start the day, and I want all my days to get a good start. Breakfast is *important,* because it helps me do better all day long.

There are both good and bad breakfasts. A bad breakfast looks like this:

- a sweet roll or a slice of white bread with butter
- a cup of tea

A *good* breakfast could look like this:
- a slice of whole-wheat bread with cheese
- yogurt or milk with granola
- an apple or some other fruit

Sometimes I eat hot cereal instead of granola. Stella has taught me how to cook it. Not everyone likes hot cereal – Arthur doesn't – but Stella and I think it's good. There are lots of different kinds of hot cereal: it can be made from oats, wheat, farina, or combinations of different grains. The cooking directions are always on the package. Hot cereal is easy to make and takes just a few minutes. As soon as you serve the cereal, you should put some water in the pot – it'll be much easier to wash that way.

If I've decided to have hot cereal for breakfast, I usually put some dried apricots in water to soak the night before. The next morning the apricots are plumped and soft. I cut them in small pieces and sprinkle them over the cereal. Then I add cold milk.

"Breakfast is served," I say to myself.

AFTER THIS BREAKFAST I'LL HAVE A GOOD DAY

INDEX